D1067637

37653000753718
Main Library: 1st floor
FIC BICKHAM
All the days were summer

✓

  FEB 86

CENTRAL ARKANSAS LIBRARY SYSTEM
LITTLE ROCK PUBLIC LIBRARY
700 LOUISIANA
LITTLE ROCK, ARKANSAS

All the Days
Were Summer

Also by Jack M. Bickham

BAKER'S HAWK
TWISTER
THE WINEMAKERS
EXCALIBUR DISASTER
DINAH, BLOW YOUR HORN
THE REGENSBURG LEGACY

All the Days Were Summer

Jack M. Bickham

DOUBLEDAY & COMPANY, INC.
GARDEN CITY, NEW YORK
1981

CENTRAL ARKANSAS LIBRARY SYSTEM
LITTLE ROCK PUBLIC LIBRARY
700 LOUISIANA STREET
LITTLE ROCK, ARKANSAS 72201

Library of Congress Cataloging in Publication Data
Bickham, Jack M.
    All the days were summer.
    SUMMARY: In the summer of 1943, as a 12-year-old boy
tries to cope with his dog's blindness and his father's
new job with German prisoners of war, he finds his life
unalterably changing.
    [1. Moving, Household—Fiction. 2. Dogs—Fiction.
3. Prisoners of war—Fiction] I. Title.
PS3552.I3S5   [Fic]
ISBN: 0-385-17597-3
Library of Congress Catalog Card Number 80-2895

Copyright © 1981 by Jack Bickham
PRINTED IN THE UNITED STATES OF AMERICA
FIRST EDITION
ALL RIGHTS RESERVED

All the Days Were Summer

1

In my heart, all the days of my youth were summer. And the summer that always dominates, the summer of my revolt against my father, of all the terrible things that happened, of my German friend—the summer of my Skipper—was in 1943.

It was in the spring of that year that my father told us one night at the supper table that we were moving to the country. He tried to say it casually, his lean face lit by a little smile, as if he were announcing a picnic. But his hand holding a fork was shaking ever so slightly and so I knew it was a momentous decision for him. My mother appeared calm. But for my sister Aggie and me there had been no warning. We were equally stunned.

Aggie, seven, had been taking a drink of her milk. She almost dropped it, and when she managed to put it down, she had a wide milk mustache that made her look even more shocked. "The country!" she gasped. "You mean leave *home?*"

"We'll have a new home," my father told her. The smile remained on his lips but I could see the strain in his face. He was tall, thin, his dark hair combed straight back, suspenders broad and dark against his white office shirt, his navy-and-white dotted bow tie askew. "It's a nice little house, Agatha, and there are trees—a little orchard—ten whole acres—and we'll have a big Victory Garden this summer. Won't you like that?"

Aggie stared at him and her big eyes welled up. "I like it *here!*" she said, and began to bawl.

My father looked like he had been shot. "Oh, now—" he began.

My mother stepped in sternly. "That's all right, George." She addressed herself to Aggie. "That's enough of that, young lady. You just sit up and eat your green beans."

"I don't *like* green beans!" Aggie wailed. "And I don't like it in the country! There are lions and bears in the country!"

"Cows, too," I said. I couldn't resist. "Vicious ones that bite."

"Danny!" Mother snapped. She was the loveliest woman in the world, blond, with vivid blue eyes, and I adored her. But when her amazing eyes glinted as they did now, I knew to shut up. She leaned over Aggie and said something more to her. Aggie started straightening up. Mother gave her her spoon. Aggie put some beans in her mouth as if they were hemlock.

"Now that's better," my mother said, giving me another dirty look. "It's a nice little house out there. We'll clean it up and it will be wonderful. We're all going to have a very nice time, *aren't* we, Danny!"

"Yes, ma'am," I said. Aggie spit the beans out in her hand and hid them behind the rim of her plate, but no one else saw it.

"What it's all about," my father told me, "is that I'm taking a new job. I don't know if you know it or not, Danny, but we're starting to get some German prisoners of war in this country now—"

"He doesn't understand that, George," my mother said softly.

"I'm *twelve!*" I protested. "I understand *all* about it!"

My father grinned. "Anyway, there's a new prisoner-of-war camp going in down south of Columbus, near the little town of

Harmony. They needed some people, and I applied. I'm going to be supervisor of the guards," he said with quiet pride.

"You mean you're going in the Army?"

"No," he said with the faintest expression of irritation. Although he was almost forty, and some vague physical complaint having to do with the inner ear had made him ineligible for the draft, he had always felt odd about being home when so many others were away at war. I instantly regretted saying something that brought this up. But he went on, "There will be a few soldiers. But most of the guards will be civilians . . . some full time, some part time. And I'll supervise all of them. It's a big, responsible job, Danny."

"You'll be great at it," I told him.

"I hope so. I hope we'll all like it. We might even get a chance to buy the farm and house later, if things work out."

"Boy!" I said enthusiastically. "It sounds real dangerous!"

"Now you sound like your mother. It isn't going to be dangerous at all. You see, they screen the prisoners. Any hard-core Nazis they put in a camp with heavy security. But these prisoners are just ordinary soldiers who have been captured. Most of them won't be bad types at all." He frowned. "Of course they are still the enemy, but . . ."

"When do we move?" I asked.

"Next week."

This was even more startling. "Next week! What about school?"

"Well, there's a nice school in Harmony, Danny. You and Agatha will just transfer in there and not miss more than a day or two."

I sat back in my chair. Supper was roast and potatoes with brown gravy, always my favorite, but even that didn't look so good all of a sudden. I thought about my pals at school. I wondered who would get my school traffic-guard badge.

"Will I get to see any of the firing squads?" I asked dubiously.

My father's head jerked. *"Firing squads!"*

"When some of those Krauts get out of line."

"Danny!" my mother exclaimed, shocked.

"Well, Mom, they're *enemies*. There isn't any German that's any good. They're all just a bunch of killers."

"Now, Squirt," my father said in his lecture tone, "that just isn't the way you ought to look at this at all. These are prisoners. They fought in the German Army and they got captured. They're people just like the rest of us."

I stared at him in consternation. "Dad. I told you: I *understand*. These guys ran over Poland and blitzkrieged France and bombed London and everything else. I know what kind of people Germans are. If you're a good American, you hate 'em—and the Japs even more."

"That's not so," my father told me. "There's such a thing as the Geneva Convention. It—"

"It says you treat prisoners decent so they'll maybe treat your people decent if they get captured," I piped up. "But it doesn't say you've got to not hate their guts."

"That kind of talk is out of line," he said sharply.

"I know what Germans are like."

"I said that would be enough!"

I avoided his eyes. He was not making any sense at all. I knew my duties as a good citizen, and hating Germans and Japanese was part of them. My father's sudden soft talk about them was dismaying—confusing.

"We'll have a very normal life down there," he said.

Puzzled and at a loss, I did not reply.

"It's a nice school down there," my father added, watching me. "You'll fit right in, both of you. And Agatha, you've wanted a cat. I imagine we'll be able to have several cats on a farm. And Danny, I know you've wanted a dog. Well, on ten acres we'll probably *need* a good dog, don't you think?"

A dog had always been one of my dreams, but it had been forbidden on a tiny city lot. Aggie had dragged home half-a-dozen cats at one time or another, but the real owners had always indignantly reclaimed them. At the mention of cats, she brightened up immediately. My reaction, although I hid it, was the opposite. This sounded like a bribe to me. And that meant all this was not so peaches-and-cream as my father and mother were letting on. I wondered what they were hiding from us.

But Aggie saw none of it. She began babbling happily about kittens, all thought of uprooting forgotten. Girls—especially girls of seven—were so dumb! It was another curse of being almost a man—of having some long pants and still some knickers —to be able to see through things like this. I almost wished I were not so sophisticated.

On the next Sunday, when we visited the new farm for the first time, it seemed an enormous journey. We left our double on Columbus' west side and drove all the way downtown, over the river and past the A.I.U. Building, said to be one of the tallest skyscrapers in Ohio, and then south on High Street. We finally got out of the city and turned on a side road and drove for another long time. We drove slowly because our 1936 Chevrolet was using a lot of oil, and oil was almost as hard to get as gas. A cool gray rain began, forcing us to close the car windows on the intoxicating fragrances of the greening fields. Finally we drove into a little town with a brick street that thrummed under the tires, great elms forming a tunnel-like canopy over the pavement. There were a great many very old, tall houses with big front porches, and some newer ones. The downtown did not strike me as much: a few stores and filling stations, a bank, a post office, one motion picture theater, a couple of grain elevators, some bumpy railroad track, and a greenhouse with a sign in the window: LOOSE LIPS SINK SHIPS.

"Well, what did you think of Harmony?" my father asked.

"Not much," I said honestly.

"Why, it looks like a very nice place," my mother said.

"You didn't see nearly all of it from the main street," my father added. "We'll explore more later."

I looked at Aggie. She had slumped back on the seat, eyes glazed, her middle two fingers in her mouth. She didn't suck her fingers except when she was upset.

After a few more miles we crossed a metal bridge over a creek or river and then slowed. Trees lined the narrow road. I saw some broad farm fields in the distance. Then we came to a gravel driveway and, beyond it through some trees, a small white house. My father turned carefully in. We parked in front of the house, which was one story, with a big front porch and a green composition roof. The rain had abated. We got out.

The first thing that struck me was the stillness. Except for distant wind and the cry of birds, there was nothing: no traffic, no voices from next door, no radios, no trucks . . . just—*quiet*. It seemed spooky.

My father took us up onto the porch of the house and produced some keys. He swung back the creaky front screen and unlocked the door. We went in.

We went into a large vacant room, the living room. Its bare wood floor was dusty, the pale yellow wallpaper faded. A few water stains showed in the paper on the ceiling. Beyond this room was another, the dining room, with a door to the back going to the kitchen and a hallway to the right leading to bedrooms. In the kitchen the linoleum was broken and the cabinets had been painted a garish yellow-green. My father kept up a running commentary.

"Have to repaint in here, of course . . . fix the cabinet doors. Looks like we might need some new washers in those faucets, too. Stove ought to clean up all right, though. Say, won't this enclosed porch be nice for storage? Now through here, kids, we've got the bathroom and the bedrooms. Agatha, this one is yours. You'll get to see the road, isn't that neat? Danny, this one is for you. You'll have plenty of space for your model airplanes . . ."

I followed numbly. In truth, the house looked horrible. It had not been well cared for, and everything was filthy and in need of repair. The windows in my room looked as though they hadn't been washed in a hundred years, and I could just *guess* who was going to get to try to make them shine again. The room was larger than my one in the city, but I didn't like it. It was too . . . square or something.

"A little new wallpaper in the bathroom will do wonders for it, Elizabeth. Really. That rust in the bowl will clean right up. Country well water does that, eh? Nothing to worry about. And look at this linen closet here! Imagine all that space, will you? I'll just repair the shelving and give it a coat of paint . . ."

Outside, we explored like troopers from a foreign land.

There was a small barn with rock walls, some hay inside. Fallen fence marked an old garden plot. Struggling through weeds, I found some cherry and apple and peach trees, and some strawberries and raspberries. The latter I discovered the hard way, by getting tangled up in their stickers.

"Get out of there, Danny!" my mother called from beyond the thicket.

"I want to go on down and see the creek!"

"All right, but be careful. And hurry. We're going back." With that she took Aggie's hand and turned up the weedy slope toward the distant house; my father walked with them.

I got out of the stickers and went on down the hill. I could hear water and smell it. Elms and maples formed a canopy overhead. I climbed over a fallen tree, startling a cottontail who hopped away on a zigzag course. My heart thumping in startlement, I watched him out of sight. If I got a dog, I thought, I could hunt with my BB gun.

Farther downslope I came to the creek, a stream about ten feet wide and only a few inches deep rippling over yellow earth and pebbles, with high, raw earth banks shaggy at the lips with winter-killed vegetation. A Baltimore oriole flew in fright from a tree as I half climbed and half fell down the bank, tumbling a spray of loose earth into the water. I accidentally stepped into the water with my right foot, going into ooze over the shoetop. The water was shockingly cold. *Now* I was in trouble, I thought, but my fascination with a real creek—and being alone in such wilderness—made worry a distant thing.

I walked along the edge of the water. Spiders scampered in the sunlight and a frog startled me again by flopping heavily into the water at my approach. In the distance somewhere I heard the mournful cry of a dove. The light wind rustled the winter-stripped trees. There were still dark rain clouds nearby, and I heard thunder. I found a piece of rotted timber and examined it carefully, dug up some bottle caps, and found an old medicine bottle which I threw and broke against a rock. I was having a great time, but the thunder repeated and I knew it was time to get back.

The banks were vertical where I stood and I did not think

I could climb out. Walking ahead in search of an easier way, I turned a slight bend in the creek and saw to my astonishment something new: jutting out of the earthen wall of the creek on my side was a large concrete drainage pipe. It was about five feet in diameter, and had a steady trickle of water issuing from it into the creek. It was high enough on the wall that the water tumbled down about three feet before making crystalline sparkles in the creek where it fell.

I scrambled up to the big pipe and craned my neck to peer inside. It seemed to go back into the earth *forever*. Dank, frightening air issued from those depths. It was pitch black in there.

I got a knee on the rough concrete lip and heaved myself into the pipe. Awkwardly straddling the stream that burbled from the depths, I took a few confident steps inward. The cold closed around me. Ahead I could see nothing whatsoever. *Be brave,* I told myself sternly, and kept going. It was mandatory to explore this!

Each step became more difficult. I began to think about the strange odor of the air inside the pipe. Sewer gas? Would they find my skeleton in here about a month from now?

I looked back the way I had come. The sunny opening looked a mile away, and very tiny. I had come farther than I had realized, and panic hit me. *What if the thing collapsed?*

Waddling to straddle the little stream, I hurried back toward the circle of daylight. When I reached it and tumbled out onto the creek bank, it was with a sense of intense relief. I looked back at the pipe's mouth while my nerves began to return to normal.

This, I thought, promised a great adventure. The pipe led *somewhere*. I would have to explore it. But I would need a flashlight, possibly string to leave behind me as a clue in case there were puzzling forks in the tunnel deeper inside.

"*Danny!*" I heard my mother calling distantly.

The bank was climbable here. I scrambled up and ran up the hill toward the house. My parents and Aggie were standing behind the house watching for me. The weeds had pulled most of the mud from my shoe where I had slipped, and they didn't notice.

"Don't go off like that," my father scolded mildly. He pointed at the clouds. "It's about to rain again. We're going."

We climbed into the car, and as we backed out the rain resumed lightly. We turned in the direction opposite the way we had come, accelerating as we went up a slight hill and passed woods on both sides of the road. We had gone less than a mile when we encountered tall, obviously new fencing on our right side. It had a strand of barbed wire along its top.

"What's that, Daddy?" Aggie piped up.

Through the trees now we could see several bleak old brick buildings on the hill, and a scattering of raw new wood construction. There were some trucks and piles of supplies.

"It used to be a private school once upon a time," my father said. "But that's the new camp now. That's where your daddy is going to work."

No one replied. The place as seen through the old trees, with the rain falling more steadily now, was grim and forboding. I did not know why at the time, but I shivered.

And they say there is no such thing as premonition.

2

The few days before we moved were filled with tension and excitement as we all packed boxes and barrels. My mother was in unfailing good spirits, and it was only when I managed to watch her unaware that I sometimes saw her pause over some picture or small item before it was packed and get a faraway look in her eyes. Some of the neighbors who were her best friends, Mrs. Jerkins and Mrs. Stein, came over often. At those times the women had coffee in the kitchen and their voices were pleasant in the house, which was rapidly becoming cavernous and drab as pictures disappeared from walls, curtains were taken down, washed, and packed, and even rugs were rolled against the day of moving. For my father the move would be momentous and a challenge. But for my mother it was going to mean shifting the focus of her universe.

My father's last day at the plant where he had spent many years was a Friday. He came home a bit early, gray-faced and worried as he walked in from the garage, but when he saw me watching him, he smiled at once. He and mother prattled about last-minute packing, being cheerful for one another. Aggie watched them awhile and seemed to sense their tensions, too. A little later I found her alone in her room, hugging her rag doll and sucking her fingers.

At school I was given an envelope of very important-looking papers to carry to Harmony. I had never been much of a figure at the school, but my moving made me a minor celebrity. For the first time I realized that the old, chalky-smelling building had been important in my life. But it was with a sense of mounting adventure that I left that following Monday for the last time, walking home alone. When I arrived, the big yellow moving van was already in front and many of our possessions had already been carried out of the house.

Aggie ran around, calling and laughing to make echoes, as the movers took out the last items. My mother diligently swept the barren floors, while my father, with me at his heels, went to the basement to make sure nothing had been forgotten. He looked at the spot where his workbench had been, then walked over to the huge cylindrical coal furnace. A faint smile on his lips, he reached down to the iron grate handle and shook it briefly, making the familiar rattling sounds that had awakened me so often on frigid winter mornings. He dusted his hands with satisfaction. "I'll never have to do that again, anyway," he told me.

"I bet you're glad," I said.

He looked at me, forehead wrinkling. "Seven years," he said.

"What?"

"We lived here seven years."

"It's the only place *I* ever remember," I admitted.

He tousled my hair. "It's going to be great on the farm. You know, Squirt, I guess I always wanted to live on a farm."

"How come you waited till you were old, then?" I asked.

"Old?" He reacted to that.

"Older, I mean," I apologized.

"I don't know." He took a deep breath. "When you're a man, you go where the work is . . . you know? I think you're too young to remember, but we've had some hard times. I've been lucky to have this job. I've gotten ahead. Maybe . . . I'm sure some people would say I'm a fool to take this chance."

"I remember when I was little," I said, "and you took your lunch to work, but there wasn't any work that day. And you came home and ate your sandwich on the kitchen table."

"You remember that, do you?"

"Yes. And your going to school at night."

He looked off into a private distance, this man I adored. "People who didn't live through the thirties will never know how it was. There were some darned thin years. I was a little lucky, getting out of the factory and into the office. They helped me a lot down there." For an instant his eyes were filled with regret and uncertainty, but then he shook himself and brightened. "Going to night school, though. That helped. A man makes his own opportunities. You should never forget that. Nobody owes you a living. You have to get ahead on your own."

"Well," I said, "that's what moving to the country is all about, isn't it?"

"That's it exactly," he said, brightening. He looked around the basement once more—at the walls that always leaked when it rained, the rusty furnace that had been his nemesis, the grimy overhead rafters—and the regret came back. He sighed again. "Come on. Let's get going."

We went upstairs. The movers were closing the big back doors of the van. Aggie was already out in the car with her doll. My father and I found my mother standing in the kitchen, looking at the space where the refrigerator had been. She was crying without sound. My father went to her and put his arms around her. She turned to cling to him. I went outside, pretending I didn't see.

By afternoon the moving van had deposited everything at the little country house, and we were all busy cleaning and unpacking. A light, cold breeze blew through the open windows and everything smelled of soap and ammonia. My father was hooking up the stove, mother was putting dishes in the repainted cabinets, and Aggie was swinging in the old porch glider while I clung to the top of the ladder in my new room, sticking pins in the wallpaper to drape kite string from wall to wall in order to hang my flying model planes. Just as I stuck one of the pins into my thumb instead of the wallpaper, the sound of a car engine came outside, and someone pounded loudly on the open front door. Holding my tongue against the hole in my thumb, I climbed down off the ladder as my father's voice and that of another man, came from the living room.

I went out just as my father introduced my mother to the man who had come to call. He was a colonel in the Army, thick-waisted and graying, with metal-framed spectacles, several service ribbons on the blouse of his dark winter uniform, gleaming brown riding boots, and a little leather quirt in one hand. Meeting my mother, he clicked his heels sharply and bowed slightly from the waist. "A pleasure, Mrs. Davidson! I look forward to working with your husband."

"It's very kind of you to call, Colonel Thatcher," my mother said solemnly.

"Think nothing of it. Think nothing of it." Colonel Thatcher's eyes roved the room, missing nothing. "You seem to be getting matters well in hand. Excellent." He spied me. "And who might you be, soldier?"

"I'm not a soldier," I told him. "I'm a civilian. I'm Danny."

He chuckled, his eyes like steel bearings. "Well, you'll be a soldier soon enough, I wager, and then the Army will make a man of you, eh?"

"No, sir. I aim to be in the Air Corps."

"The Air Corps!" He strode over to me, boots thudding, and tapped me lightly with his whip. "All right, then! Bully! Study hard in school. You'll need your education if you're to become an officer and a gentleman."

"I think OCS will take care of that," I said.

The colonel's hard eyes widened. I had the impression I sometimes got at the movies: of someone working very hard to play a part, and yet not convincing me. "You know about OCS, then, do you?" Without waiting for a reply, he turned to my parents. "A bright lad! I pity the Germans when his generation enters the fray."

"My heavens," my mother said softly. "It's not going to last *that* long . . . is it?" Her dismay was clear in her eyes.

"Popular wisdom would have a short war, now that America's industrial might has been mobilized," the colonel said heavily. "Many of us with military experience, however, view things differently. Do you have any idea, madam, how long the Germans planned for this war? Or the Japs?"

"I know we've begun to turn the tide," my mother said, worry lines showing in her forehead.

"Madam, we are dealing with fanatics here. Before Germany surrenders, air power will have to demolish their homeland. There will have to be the mightiest invasion ever mounted by man, to conquer the fortress continent. And even after all that is accomplished, we still face those yellow . . . people in the Pacific. We may be looking at a war that lasts into the 1950s!"

Mother looked at me again more fearfully. We were doing the same mental arithmetic. I imagined myself flying a P-38, shooting down hundreds of Nazi Messerschmitts. Her imaginings were clearly not as happy. "Oh, Colonel," she said, "that's a terrible prospect."

"Regardless of how long it may take," the colonel said, "we must prevail. And for those of us charged with the heavy responsibility of maintaining order on the home front—keeping rebellious prisoners in line and our homes safe for our women and children—our sense of duty must never falter." He glared at my father. "We have a big responsibility, Davidson. Working together, we can handle it."

"I hope so, sir," my father said. He looked pale and drawn.

The colonel began pacing, hands behind his back holding his quirt. "The first shipment of prisoners arrives in three days' time. My detachment is not at strength. Twenty-four enlisted men and two other officers. We have thirty-seven civilian employees on the report as of today. You'll have precious little time to shape them up, but they must be ready. I've called a general meeting for oh-eight-hundred hours tomorrow. You will be ready to begin making out duty rosters by that time, I assume?"

My father, standing there in his bib overalls and oil-stained work shirt, looked stunned. "I didn't know things were moving that fast. We just started moving in—"

"Everything has been accelerated," Colonel Thatcher snapped. "This is war. We have no choice but to be ready. I have asked for additional military men, but we will have to make do with what we have. It means all of us must expect extra duty. You understand, of course."

My father took a rag from his back pocket and began wiping his hands. "It looks like I'd better get at those rosters right away."

"Bully," the colonel said, and slapped his thigh with his quirt. "Security is of the essence, Davidson. Remember that. It's all well and good to talk about prisoners of war being treated fairly, and I intend to live up to the letter of the law of the Geneva Convention. But we must never forget. These people are still the enemy. Give them an inch and they'll take a mile. Firmness. That's the ticket. I expect to run this camp the military way. I expect no less from you or the other civilians."

"My dad will do his part," I piped up.

The colonel swung to stare at me. "Eh?"

"I said my dad will do his part, Colonel. And you can count on me, too."

"Oh, I can, eh?"

"I hate Germans," I told him proudly. "If any of them ever try to get loose, I'll help. I'm a crack shot with a BB gun. You get me a real gun, and—"

"Danny, stop it," my mother said, pale.

"Let him talk," the colonel said. "The lad has spunk. I like that." He bent over and patted my head. "Think you'd like to kill a few Krauts, do you?"

"I'll do my share," I boasted.

"Well, my boy, if we do our job properly at the camp, you'll never have to test your resolve locally. We'll keep them in line. You can be sure of that." He grinned a death's-skull grin. "Maybe we'll get to kill a few for you if we have any smart alecks in the crowd."

"Colonel," my mother said huskily, "I think this child gets quite enough talk about this terrible war."

The colonel looked sharply at her. "Of course, madam. A mother's point of view, eh? I applaud you for it." He patted me again and turned back to my father. "I expect we'll get along well. You have a lot to do. I know I can count on you. I can see you have a lot of work to do here at the house, but the war effort must take priority, eh? Our efforts are helping make the world safe for Democracy. No sacrifice is too great. As you learn my ways, we'll work together as a tight-knit team. Give me all you've got. It's for America."

"Yes, sir," my father said respectfully.

"Fine, then," the colonel said. He bowed stiffly to my mother. "I trust you will enjoy your new quarters, madam." He walked to the door, then turned back to my father. "Oh. I suppose you have no piece for your own use?"

"Piece?" my father repeated blankly.

"Weapon. Sidearm."

"No. I—"

"One will be issued. Good day."

We stood at the front windows and watched him walk out to his jeep, where a young corporal waited behind the wheel. The colonel vaulted heavily into the rear seat. The corporal started the engine and backed out. The jeep went down the road. Two little flags with silver eagles on them fluttered on the front fenders. I looked at my parents and felt embarrassment for them. It had always been my curse, even as a child, to see through some of the sham the world presented, and the colonel had not impressed me. He was a cruel man, I thought, and perhaps dangerous. Stupid men intent on appearances were often dangerous. I wished my mother and father had not been subjected to this performance.

My mother looked only worried. My father was grim. "Well," he said finally.

"Are you really going to carry a *gun*?" my mother asked.

"Oh, maybe not," he said. "And if I do, it will just be for appearances' sake. There's no danger, Elizabeth! I told you that."

"That's not what he just said, George."

"Well, he's an army man. You know how they are in the Army."

She looked at him, clearly uncertain and frightened. Then her shoulders slumped. "I'd better get back to the kitchen." She turned and walked out of the room. My father looked after her for what seemed a long time, then followed.

I went back to work in my room. After a little while, Aggie came in, dragging a very old, small flannel blanket and sucking her fingers. She stood watching me.

"If you don't stop that," I said, "you'll get buck teeth. How many times do you have to be told?"

"Don't care," she said around her fingers.

"Aggie, you're in school now, for cripe's sake! Grow up!"

She looked at me with those big eyes and started to cry without sound. Instantly contrite, I went over and knelt beside her, hugging her. "Hey. There's nothing to be scared of. School will be just fine."

"Nobody will like me," she sniffled.

"Hey! *Everybody* will like you! How could they help it? You're a really neat girl."

"I'm not neat," she said. "I'm *little*. I wanted to stay in Columbus. I don't like this house and I don't like the country and I don't like a new school and I don't like that mean man that was here and I don't like *anything!*"

"Just listen here," I told her. "Dad's got a nice new job here. He's working for our *country*. It's going to be great here. We'll have lots of neat new stuff to do. And," I added, providing the clincher, "we *got* to be good. It's our patriotic duty to help Mom and Dad."

Aggie looked at me. "What's patriotic mean?"

"Well, it's . . . uh . . . where you do what you need to for your country, for America, and you fight guys that are against it."

"I don't want to fight," Aggie said. "I just want to be in Columbus!"

"Well, you're not in Columbus, so you might as well shape up," I said crossly, losing patience with her.

She began sniffling again.

"Dad is going to be guarding Germans, Aggie. *Germans*. The enemy. The meanest guys in the world, except for maybe the Japs. Stop feeling sorry for yourself and think about hating Germans and Japs, if you want to act like a real American."

"I don't even know any Germans," she protested. "I don't know how to hate good anyway. I'm *little*."

"Well, it's time to start acting like a grownup. Learn!"

"It won't do any good," she sighed. "I've already tried. I *know* it's important to guard mean old Germans. But I'm lonesome."

I saw a different tack was necessary. "Aggie, do you know how Dad always used to come home from the plant tired?"

She put her fingers in her mouth and watched me with those big eyes. "Yes," she said, muffled.

"And then he'd sit at the supper table and tell Mom how all sorts of stuff went wrong at work? How sometimes later he'd just sit there and smoke his cigarette and look like he was a million miles off?"

"Yes."

"Well, he's gotten away from that plant now, Aggie. If you aren't big enough to hate Germans right, then think of Dad. He's got a better chance with this new job. He's *quit* Columbus, probably forever. He and Mom have enough to worry about without us acting like dumb kids. We've got to act big."

"Why?" she asked protestingly.

"Because we owe it to Mom and Dad!"

"Everyone wants me to act big," Aggie wailed, "but I haven't even had a chance to be *little* very long yet!"

It was a cry of sheer protest. I remember it so vividly because in later years I was to hear so many adults say the same kind of thing from vastly different perspective. In our time, we knew as children that part of our duty was to grow up as swiftly as possible, to be responsible citizens for the sake of our parents. Our obligations even when very young were stressed to us, and they were grave. Our parents—much less the world—did not owe us a living. It was up to us to live up to our parents, obey their code, become adults, good soldiers.

We did as we were told, and not without pain. But it was the way things were done.

Then, however, as we really did become adults, the voices from on high sounded different. Problems of the children, we were told, were the fault of parents. It was up to us to be responsible for our offspring. We owed them freedom and a carefree existence, and patience if they told us that our way of life was now obsolete. The rules had been changed; now it was the elders who owed obedience to their children. Again, it was up to us to be good soldiers.

So we tried. But now the shadows begin to lengthen across the parade ground and still we stand at attention, doing our duty, hearing the sounds of distant laughter. We seldom speak out because that would be against the regulations as we were taught—and believed—them. But inside us a voice cries. *Hey, everybody! Wait! Somehow we missed our turn!*

At the time, of course, I knew none of this. I consoled Aggie, and after a while she smiled, rubbing on her blanket, kissed me, and padded off to bed. It was getting late. I put on my own pajamas.

That night I awakened many times, sitting upright from some vague dream and confused about where I was in this new room of strange shadows and unknown dimensions. Every time, as I came to reality, I saw the dim light coming down the hallway from the kitchen, where my father sat hunched over rosters and ledger sheets, preparing for the morning. At 6 A.M. my mother awakened me and Aggie and nagged us into getting washed and dressed for school. The bus came by the house at 7:20, and we boarded. My mouth was dry. Every face on the bus was, of course, that of a stranger. Aggie squeezed my hand so tight it hurt. For all of us, our new lives had begun.

No one spoke to us on the bus that morning. There was a minimum of fooling around—a couple of older boys wrestling over a yo-yo, another grabbing a girl's lunch and throwing it to the back of the bus, and all the older girls giggling. Aggie and I sat near the front, eyes to the front. The driver, an old man named Mr. Cline, good-naturedly let the horsing around escalate until the lunch was thrown; then he turned and gave a single glare that silenced everyone.

The bus finally trundled into Harmony, past a little city building and some garages I hadn't seen earlier, across a bridge over the Big Walnut, the broad, slow-flowing river that dissected the town, and into the graveled parking area beside a long, low, modern-looking school building with lots of glass. There were kids of all ages everywhere. Aggie and I got off the bus. Mr. Cline nudged me, pointing to a green metal door in the side of the school building.

"In there," he said. "The office is just to the right. You're new, ain't you?"

Thanking him, I dragged Aggie inside. The gleaming halls smelled of wax. In the large office area, several women were bustling around. I got someone's attention and handed over our papers. After some consultations, one of the ladies took Aggie's hand. "Come with me, dear, and we'll introduce you to your new teacher. My, that's a pretty dress!" Aggie went off, looking like she was being taken to the electric chair. I continued to wait. There was enormous bustle in the halls outside, and then they began to clear and quiet. I sat down on a straight chair against the wall. Everyone seemed to disappear. It got quiet. I waited. Finally a tall woman with gray hair came out of an inner office and looked at me.

"What are you still doing here?" she demanded.

"Waiting," I said.

"For *what?*"

"Well, for someone to tell me where to go."

She scowled at some papers. "You're the new boy. Davidson. You're supposed to be in room one-twenty. You'd better hurry. Land! You're already late!"

I hesitated. "One-twenty?"

"That way," she said severely, pointing. "Hurry. You're in trouble, boy!"

I rushed out, heading the direction indicated. All the doors to classrooms were closed and I didn't see a soul. From behind one door I heard them doing the Pledge of Allegiance. Sweat bolted out of every pore on my body. I found Room 118 and turned a corner looking for 120, and there stood Benny Harrison.

Not that I knew him then, of course. But I knew he was someone important. He was standing beside a closed door, leaning against the wall, one booted foot behind him resting on the wall. He was not large, only a bit taller than I, and slender. But everything about him said *Tough!* He was wearing a tight pale-blue tee shirt and short pants, cut-offs, with lace-up boots that almost reached the knee. I had never seen anyone wear battered lace-up boots with short pants before. He had a round beanie-type hat on his head and it had badges and trinkets sewed all over it. He was picking his teeth with the small blade of a pocketknife.

He turned narrowed eyes to me, saying nothing.

"Is this one-twenty?" I asked breathlessly, pointing to the door with the numbers 120 on the opaque glass.

"What's it look like, stupid?"

I reached for the doorknob. He stopped me with the hand that still held the knife. "Where do you think you're going?"

"In there," I said, "sir."

"What's your name?"

"Danny Davidson."

"You're new here."

"Yes, sir."

He stared at me for a long moment. I chilled to the soles of my feet. There was nothing but violence and hate behind those icy eyes. I didn't move a muscle while he seemed to think about it.

Finally he let his hand drop. "Okay."

I opened the door and went in. Sunlight flooded the room from windows on the far side. The room was golden with the light, and the walls were clean white, the floor gleaming wood, the desks modern blond of the type that let you slide in from the side and write on an arm, rather than the lift-up bench types we had had in the city. A sea of faces turned toward me, and at the front of the room a large woman paused in what she had been saying. She was gray and massive, with the face of George Washington.

"Yes?" she said.

"I'm Danny Davidson," I croaked.

"You're late," she snapped. "That's not a very good start, is it?"

"No, ma'am."

"Come over here."

I approached the bench. *Everyone* was watching, judging me. My flesh crawled.

"Class," the woman said, a hand heavy on my shoulder, "we have a new member. This is Danny Davidson and he comes to us from the Columbus schools. Danny, suppose you introduce yourself to the class."

I looked at her, strangled. "Ma'am?"

"Tell your new classmates something about yourself!"

"Well, I—my parents and I live in the country—"

Someone snickered and there was general shuffling. Sweat stung my eyes. "We just moved, see. My dad—"

"No, no, no. What about *you?*"

"Me?"

"What are you like? What do you do? What do you want to become?"

"Well . . ." My mind raced. All I could see was the blur of the faces. I had to say *something*. "I—I guess I like school all right. I make model airplanes. I listen to the radio a lot. I'm a great football player because of my exceptional speed—" There were some louder snickers, and all the girls were grinning and nudging each other. I stopped, realizing how stupid I had sounded.

"What do you play?" the teacher asked helpfully.

"Ma'am?" My mind had shut off entirely. I wished I were dead.

"Play!" She smiled. "What do you play?"

"Well, I've got a mouth harp—"

The room erupted in laughter. Startled, I felt it beat down around me. Over it, the teacher chuckled, "In football, Danny! What *position* do you play?"

Horribly mortified, I saw how I had erred. "Halfback," I choked.

"Good. I'm your new teacher, Mrs. Broadus. Now—"

The door opened from the hall. My earlier antagonist came in, feet shuffling, knife still picking at his teeth. Mrs. Broadus whirled, fire in her eye. "Benny Harrison, get that hat off your head!"

Benny took his beanie off and tossed it on the floor. He

stepped on it, staring insolently back at her. There were snickers.

"Now pick it up and get to your desk! And put that knife away!"

Benny obeyed, slouching down a far aisle. He took a playful swing at a smaller boy who almost fell off his desk seat dodging the blow. Benny reached his desk and slumped into it, one booted foot cocked on the edge of the writing surface.

"Sit up right!" Mrs. Broadus snapped. He obeyed again, giving her his killing look.

Mrs. Broadus sighed and returned her attention to me. "You see that empty desk over under the windows? That's your place." I went to the appointed desk and sat down gratefully.

"Now," Mrs. Broadus said. "We were starting to talk about our geography lesson. Can anyone tell me what the main crop is in Brazil?"

There was a moment's silence. "Brazil nuts?" Benny Harrison asked hollowly.

Mrs. Broadus whirled to her desk and picked up a heavy yardstick. "Up here," she ordered, pointing to a tall stool in the front corner.

Benny Harrison slouched up the aisle. He climbed onto the stool, hat in hand. Mrs. Broadus went to a nearby table and picked up a dunce cap made of construction paper. She went over and rammed it on top of Benny Harrison's head with enough force to shake him. "Now sit there and be quiet!"

Benny Harrison sat impassive, staring out at the class. Mrs. Broadus, after glaring at him a while longer, returned to her desk, turning her back to him. He removed the dunce cap and put on his beanie. Mrs. Broadus pretended she didn't see. I didn't blame her. He was the toughest kid I had ever seen.

At first recess I went down the hall and located Aggie's room and saw her happily playing with some girls her own age in the playground just outside. Satisfied that she was all right, I would have preferred to find a hole to crawl into rather than go on out and face my peers, but signs at the doors said *everyone* would exercise outdoors except during bad weather. The air was cool but by no stretch of the imagination could the weather be considered bad. I went out to meet my fate.

It was a large playground, the near end paved between the school and the adjoining gymnasium building, then an area of gravel where there were swings and teeter-totters for the small children, and then a vast expanse of well-worn grass. The smaller tots were swinging and teeter-tottering and running around. The seventh-graders stayed close to the buildings, the boys standing around and acting tough and the girls giggling a lot. I saw that my grade—the sixth—had scattered out on the grassy field, the girls running and tossing a ball and the boys starting a game of capture the flag. As I watched, a fifth-grader darted the long length of the field, grabbed the blue rag off a tree limb, and raced back through chasing sixth-graders across the center line and into his celebrating teammates. The rag was then dutifully run to the fifth-grade end of the field and stuck on a bush.

At this point rough hands grabbed me by both arms and propelled me away from the building and out across the playground toward the game. Looking around frantically, I saw that I had been grabbed by two of my classmates, a stocky, sandy-haired boy a few inches taller, and an even bigger, lankier kid with pimples whose name was Inright. I knew from observation that morning in class that they were the ringleaders of the class, the dominant boys, if Benny Harrison were left out of the equation.

"Lemme go!" I said, struggling as they bore me along toward a shady spot between buildings.

"Just shuddup," the stockier boy growled, "and maybe you won't get hurt."

There was no sense in fighting them. They hauled me down the side of the building and in under a metal fire escape from the upper level of the gym. It was an isolated spot and they pushed me against the wall.

"I'm Sheehan," the stockier boy said. "This is Inright. Now. What do you think you're doing here?"

"I'm going to school here," I said, scared.

"Where are you from?"

"Columbus."

"Where in Columbus?"

"The west side."

"Where on the west side?"

"Clarendon School."

Sheehan sneered. "I guess you think you're tough."

"No."

"I guess you think you're some kind of a stud, coming from Columbus down here with the country yokels."

"No!"

Sheehan reached out and got a handful of my shirt. "Let me get a few things straight with you. We don't like kids from Columbus. You get out of line here, and we'll beat the tar out of you. You're on probation. You understand?"

I struggled. My shirt tore. Some instinct took over. I hit Sheehan in the face. It was not a hard blow, but he was so shocked that he let me go. Inright growled and lunged at me. I ducked him and ran. They came right behind me. Now they were going to kill me. I raced headlong around the corner of the building, heading for safety in numbers, and skidded to a halt. Standing there in front of me was Benny Harrison.

I stopped, sure I was dead. Benny Harrison stared slit-eyed at me, legs spread, hands on his hips. Behind me, Sheehan and Inright thundered into view. They too saw Benny and stopped. He stared at them. They froze for a count of three or four, then turned and fled without a word.

Benny Harrison had not moved. His gimlet eyes swiveled to mine. "Okay, kid. You're saved."

I stared at him in wonder. I could only utter the uppermost thought: *"Why?"*

"Why what?" he snapped.

"Why did you save me?"

"You punched Sheehan. He's bigger than you. I liked that." Relief flooded through me. "Thanks! I really—"

"On the other hand," Benny Harrison cut in coldly, "maybe I just wanted to save you for myself." He ejected a little spit from between his teeth. "I'll think about it." Behind him the school bell sounded. *"You* better hurry," he said in a tone that clearly implied the worlds of difference between us.

I hurried. Class had been resumed about ten minutes when he sauntered in.

3

In Columbus, my afternoons had often followed a pattern. I got home from school in time to change clothes and sit down at my desk, covered with a sheet of cardboard, and work on the current flying model while listening to the Zenith. Stella Dallas and Lorenzo Jones were among my favorites, and helped provide a time reference while I cut out and pinned tiny balsa-wood members to the model blueprint, always using more fragrant airplane glue than I should have. At five, Jack Armstrong came on.

In the country, however, it was clear the pattern would be different. The bus did not get Aggie and me back home until after four. My room, like much of the house, was still a wreck. Our mother met us at the door with cookies and a list of orders. The new Stuka model was going to have to wait.

Supper was ready as usual at six, but my father did not drive in until almost seven. He came in the back door, smiling cheerfully. He looked wilted and worn down. He kissed my mother. "Everything all right?" he asked.

"Fine," she said. "Hurry and wash. Supper is ready."

He took a deep breath. "What a day. Whew! I'll hurry."

At the supper table he told Mother about it, and Aggie and I listened. The camp was going to be physically ready, he said, assuming the plumbers worked all night. He had met with the army officers and all the civilian guards. They were going to be short-handed, and the drivers of the trucks that would take prisoners around area farms to do work would also have to double as watchmen.

"It's really a massive puzzle," my father said, frowning. "The colonel says we'll never have as many men as we really ought to have. I not only have to make out the duty rosters, plan sick fill-ins, and make sure all the spots are covered; I have to write up the rules and regulations, devise an accounting system, formulate methods for keeping track of all the prisoners by name, and start trying to devise books that will make sure we rotate work to the various farms in an equitable way." He shook his head. "I'm afraid starting the garden will have to wait awhile, honey."

"We'll start on the garden," my mother said. "Don't worry about that."

"I'll get everything organized, honey, and then you won't have to bear such a load."

"That's all right. You have plenty to do."

They looked at each other, Aggie and me forgotten.

"I still think I did the right thing," my father told her.

"Of course you did."

"When Finnegan got the promotion, there wasn't anything else I could do."

"I know, I know."

"This could lead to something, Elizabeth. I can grow in this job. I can move up in the government service. And I'm *doing* something for the war effort. It isn't much, but it's something. I'm not just a . . . 4-F."

"You were never just a 4-F."

"My draft card—"

"You were *never* just a 4-F," my mother repeated, her bright eyes angry. "You went to that company as a stocker, part time, and you worked hard and studied at night and learned accounting. You *worked* your way into the office. Without you, they could never have changed production to bayonets that quickly. Even if you hadn't had your health problem, they would have had to keep you out of the service to help keep that company together. Now you're going to be even more important. I don't ever want to hear that 4-F talk again!"

He stared at her, his tired face slack, and then slowly he smiled. "Hey," he said. "Do you know what?"

"What?" she asked crossly.

"You're great. Do you know that?"

It was her turn to flush and smile. "Eat your supper."

He turned to me. "How was school today?"

"Fine," I lied.

"Nice kids?"

"Sure."

"You'd better eat up," he told me. "We have a little errand to run later."

"Errand?" I echoed.

"Well," he said slowly, "it seems that the colonel's female shepherd had some puppies. They're weaned now."

I stared at him and my heart began thumping. "Yeah?"

"Yeah," he said, watching me closely. "So I thought . . . if you wanted to . . . we might drive back over to the post after supper, and look the pups over. Maybe, if you find one you like, we could bring it home."

"*Yow!*" I yelled.

My mother dropped her fork. "Don't ever scream like that at the supper table again!" But she was laughing when she said it.

Aggie looked disgusted. "When do I get my kitten?" she asked.

My father's grin threatened to split his face. "I thought you'd never ask, Agatha."

We all looked at him. He continued to gaze at my little sister. "Maybe, if you were to go out and check the box in the back seat of the car, you might find something to interest you."

Aggie's eyes widened. Then she was off the chair like a bolt. The back screen door slammed as she rocketed out.

"You didn't," my mother said.

"I did," my father said.

Outside, Aggie started squealing with delight. Moments later she exploded back into the kitchen. Under each arm was a furry gray ball with staring eyes and a swishy tail.

"Oh, Daddy, *Daddy!*" she cried, running to him.

One of the kittens squirmed and jumped onto the table.

"Don't let it get on the table!" Mother said. "Don't let it—watch out! it's—" Aggie's milk was turned over. Mother ran for a towel. The other kitten got loose and ran under the stove. It was happy pandemonium.

After supper, my father helped with the dishes as usual. Aggie played with her kittens and I squirmed. I could hardly believe it. I was actually going to get a dog. Even when my father had mentioned it in Columbus, it had seemed only a mythic possibility. But now it was *real*. The entire farm suddenly looked better to me.

Finally the dishes were finished. My father came into the living room and sat down in his favorite chair and took out his pack of Chesterfields. He removed one, examined it, and tapped it sharply three times on the back of his hand. Then he lit it with his small aluminum lighter and leaned back. This was all part of his ritual. In Columbus he had looked at the paper with his evening cigarette. Here the paper didn't get delivered, so he watched his smoke drift across the room. He looked tired. I sat quiet, waiting. My mother came in and sat opposite him and picked up the latest copy of *Liberty*. Aggie was off in the back of the house somewhere, squealing with her kittens.

"We'll have to get a dirt box," my father said.

"Are we going to keep them in the house?" my mother asked.

"Well, for a little while, Elizabeth. Part of the time."

She sighed. "You know how I am about the house."

"I know. But if we let kittens out right away, they'll wander off."

"Will we have to have his puppy in the house too?"

"We'll put him in that big carton from out back, the one we had the dishes in. Just temporarily."

"I just don't want hairs all over everything," my mother said, her face strained. "People come to call and they see mess everywhere." She stopped, and her face struggled. "Although I don't know who will be coming to see us out here." She began, shockingly, to cry.

My father stabbed the Chesterfield out in the ash stand and went over to kneel beside her chair. "Hey," he said softly, stroking her arm.

"I'm sorry," she said, still crying.

"It's going to be all right, babe. We'll meet people here—"

She clung to him. I was enormously distressed. "Mom, I don't have to have a dog. I don't even want a dumb old dog!"

She looked up at me, smiling through the tears. "Oh, honey, it isn't the dog. It isn't anything at all."

"You're *crying!*"

"I'm just tired, honey." She held out her arms to me and I fled into them. She was fragrant and wonderful. "You just run along and get your puppy and I'll be just fine. Mothers are just a little silly sometimes."

"I'll keep him real clean, Mom. I'll make him stay in his box and teach him to mind and he'll be a good watchdog and bark if anybody comes in the day when we're at school and he'll be real nice for all of us, I *promise!*"

She dried her eyes. "Of course he will, of course he will." She laughed a little. "Now hadn't you two men better go *get* that puppy, instead of sitting here talking about him?"

"I guess that's right," my father said, still upset. "Ready to go, Squirt?"

"I sure am!" I told him.

"We won't be gone long," he promised my mother, and I followed him out through the kitchen to the waiting car.

Darkness had come on. My father started the car and turned on the lights that made the big oval of the instrument panel glow, then eased the gear shift into low and released the clutch slowly, gentling the big machine into motion. I had never seen him mistreat any piece of machinery, and the car was the object of his gentlest attentions. We pulled out onto the road, accelerating easily. The lights of the house faded behind us.

"Don't be upset, Squirt," he told me. "Moving is hard on big people. But your mother is all right."

"I hate it when she cries. It—scares me."

He was silent on this for a moment. Finally he said, "Moving is always hard. I guess you never know for certain whether you're doing the right thing. But sometimes you've got to take a chance, Squirt. You can't just walk up to the same dead end all your life. Sometimes a man just has to take the bull by the horns."

I wasn't sure what he meant. He often said things like this that I knew were very serious, and seldom was I able fully to penetrate them. So I kept quiet, afraid I might say something dumb. There was no one in the world—not even my mother— whom I more wanted to impress and please than this man. I already knew with a wisdom deeper than years that he had battered his way upward from the most abject poverty. We were still, I suppose, very poor. But now we had an old car and we had meat sometimes for supper and I seldom went very long with cardboard in the bottoms of my shoes now. My father had accomplished all this with the work and the nights at school, which sometimes meant I saw him only briefly, at supper, for weeks at a time. Whatever he did was to me *right*. I only wished I were not so dumb and little and such a worry to him sometimes. He drove himself hard and never seemed to make a mistake. All I wanted to do was measure up to him.

"So is school all right?" he asked after a while, driving.

I thought briefly about my new enemies, Bill Sheehan and Phil Inright, and the specter of Benny Harrison. "Oh, sure," I said. "Fine."

"Fine," he repeated. "That's fine, Squirt."

We drove along new fencing, shiny in the headlights. After a while he slowed the car and we pulled into a gravel driveway. Ahead was a tall gate with barbed wire on it, and a wooden guard shack, not yet painted. From the shack marched a soldier in uniform, with a rifle. The headlights glittered on his buttons. I was impressed as hell.

My father rolled down his window as the soldier approached. "We're here to see the colonel, Sergeant."

"Yes, sir," the guard said. "You're expected, sir." He went back and swung the gate open. As we drove through, he snapped to attention and saluted.

"Wow! They salute *you*, Dad?"

My father smiled, embarrassed. "I wish they wouldn't."

"Wow! Are you in charge of the soldiers, too?"

"Well, not really, Squirt. I guess I could give them orders in a pinch. But I don't expect any pinches, really."

"Have you got a gun yet? Can I see it?"

"Oh, I've got a revolver, yes. But I just shoved it in the drawer of my desk. It's just nonsense."

"Wow! I bet those old Germans won't try anything around *here*, right?"

"Danny, it's no big thing. I hate to disillusion you, but it really isn't. These prisoners coming here are people just like you and me. They've been captured. For them the war is over. Dangerous prisoners have been screened out and sent elsewhere. I've got an idea if we left the front gate open, the prisoners would go out and close them to make sure nobody wandered off by mistake."

I stared at him as we crept along the compound road, heading for the cluster of buildings ahead. "You make it sound like it's nothing."

"We've got to shelter them," he told me slowly. "Feed them. Take care of their medical needs. Keep track of them, keep them working in the fields. It's a big job. But Danny, don't get thinking this is some kind of Tyrone Power war movie. It isn't."

I was disappointed. "Well, you'd do better in war than Tyrone Power *anyway*."

He laughed, something he seldom did. "Sure I would. Okay, pay attention now. The big wood building is the mess hall, see? These two brick ones are where the men will sleep. Over there, that's the old school gym. We'll use it as a gym, too. See the row of trucks over yonder? That's how we'll truck them to their work on the farms."

We passed the new construction and the hulking old bricks with new piping, containing new electrical work, shiny on their sides. Going around the gym, we encountered another high

fence and gate, this one standing open. Beyond this gate were
trees, lights shining through them from a distance. We drove on
gravel through the trees and came to a great old mansion of a
house with lights blazing in every window.

"This used to be the schoolmaster's house," my father explained. "The colonel lives here now." He pointed beyond the
house to another cluster of lights perhaps a hundred yards
away. "New barracks for the soldiers." He braked, halted in
front of the house with its new flagpole. "Here we are."

As we got out, the front door of the mansion opened and the
colonel came out to greet us. He was still in uniform, the jacket
off, tie gone, boots replaced by house slippers. He looked vastly
different with the slippers at the ends of skinny legs in the rid-
ing-type pants.

"Here you are, Davidson!" he said loudly. "Good!" He
turned to me. "Ready to get a good guard dog, son?"

"I thought you had puppies," I said.

He grunted a little laugh. "Ha! Yes. Pups now, and the good
Lord only knows what traveling man was the father! But
they're going to be big rascals, all of them. Make good guard
dogs." He scowled at me. "We're going to need good guard
dogs with all these Huns around here."

I didn't say anything. "Huns" were what people had called
the Germans in the other war, the first one long ago. The colonel frightened me a little, but I also saw that there was something cheaply theatrical and false about him. I didn't know how
to handle this combination of perceptions. I said nothing.

Talking rapidly about TO&E's, S-2, matériel, and other
things I didn't fully comprehend, the colonel led us into the
house and through a series of great, echoing rooms with packing crates stacked around in them. In the kitchen we met his
wife, a gray-haired woman with eyes just like his, slate. She
gave us both a wintry smile and stood back beside a half-un-
packed barrel of dishes while the colonel took us on out onto
the back porch. An enormous German shepherd bitch rose
from the shadows and barked once, making me jump clear back
into the kitchen.

"*Down,* Helge!" the colonel roared. He pointed to the far

side of the porch. "Over there!" The big dog slunk across the floor and lay down obediently, watching me with sullen eyes. The colonel went to the shadowy area where she had been and pulled something—a carton with the side cut out—into the middle of the floor. From the rug-padded carton spilled a tiny explosion of puppies.

"Look at that!" my father said, laughing.

There were five of them, three brown ones, one brown-and-white, and one almost all black. They frolicked out of the box and cavorted around the colonel's legs, yipping and rolling over one another. I bent to be engulfed by them. They ran and jumped and nipped at my hands, almost scaring me. One of them, the little black fellow, ran around in little circles, whining, not joining the others in practically engulfing me.

"Good stock," the colonel said, picking one of the brown ones up and showing it to my father. "You see the size of these paws already? They'll be good watchdogs!"

The little black puppy, running in his aimless circles, practically bumped into my leg. He stopped and sort of leaned against my foot. I reached down and picked him up. He stared at me with enormous dark eyes and whined again. I held him close. His stubby tail began to wag and his sandpapery tongue scoured my face.

"Ouch!" I giggled. "Hey! Stop that!" He only licked more frantically, wriggling as if trying to get inside my shirt.

"Running an ad in the Harmony paper Friday," the colonel said. "They'll go fast then."

I put the black puppy down and picked up a brown one. This one wiggled and nipped at my fingers playfully, hurting me slightly with his sharply pointed little milk teeth. The other pups all gamboled around the floor, rolling and wrestling. The black puppy scurried around my feet, nudging at me pitifully. I put the brown pup down and picked "my" puppy up again. He repeated his frenzied, joyful act. I got the giggles again.

"What do you think, Squirt?" my father asked, grinning.

It was no contest. "This one," I said, holding my black puppy. "*This* one!"

The colonel scowled. "Runt of the litter."

"Are you sure, son?" my father asked, also frowning.

I hugged my dog closer against me. "Yes!"

My father raised his eyebrows and sighed as if I had disappointed him. "Well, it's your dog." He reached into his pocket and took out some one-dollar bills. "There you are, Colonel."

The colonel carefully counted the three dollars and pocketed them. "You understand, Davidson, that I'll get twice that from the ones I advertise."

"Yes, sir," my father said respectfully. "We both appreciate it, don't we, Squirt?"

"Yes, sir," I said. "We sure do!"

"Think nothing of it," the colonel said grandly. With a wrist-flicking motion he glanced at his watch, worn on the underneath side of his wrist. "Almost twenty-one hundred."

"We have to be going," my father said.

"Perhaps you could stay for coffee?" the colonel's wife asked from the kitchen doorway, where she had stood witness. "It won't take a minute." She gave me a smile. "I have some cookies."

I looked at my father. He hesitated.

"I'm sure they want to get their new pup home, Gladys," the colonel said. "And it's getting late. Big day for all of us tomorrow, eh, Davidson?"

"Yes, sir," my father said. "We'd better get going, ma'am."

The colonel's wife looked disappointed. Her shoulders slumped a little as we went back through her kitchen, leaving her alone. The colonel walked us to the car, I clutching my puppy. He was quiet, a hot little bundle against my breast.

"Take good care of him, boy," the colonel told me sternly as I climbed in the car. "He'll be a good guard dog for you." He glanced across the car hood at my father. "See you bright and early, Davidson. The first trucks of prisoners are en route at this moment."

My father nodded and got in behind the wheel. We backed around and drove away. The colonel stood in the blazing lights of his doorway, legs spread, hands on his hips, skinny legs fragile-looking in the house slippers. We drove through the quadrangle of old brick buildings.

Just as we moved toward the gate, lights flashed on in the buildings behind us and an earsplitting siren began to wail. I sat up sharply. More sirens were screaming all over the area. My father slowed for the gate, where the soldier was already out.

"What *is* it?" I yelled over the racket. "What's *happening?*"

"Nothing at all," my father said easily. "Just testing the warning system again."

The soldier opened the gate for us and we drove through to another smart salute. As we moved onto the highway, the sirens continued to wail and I could look back and see distant figures running in a glare of lights. I studied my father's impassive face. "I thought you said there wasn't any danger!"

"Well, Squirt," he said softly, "you've got to practice for every eventuality, the colonel says." He glanced at me and I saw that he was embarrassed. "It's the army way."

If I had been older, or less immersed in the sheer joy of my puppy, I might have seen the trouble coming even then. But, looking back, I remember no such premonition. We went home and showed my puppy to Mother and Aggie, and brought the big box in from the back and put it in a corner of my room with an old piece of rugging in it. My father found an old pan suitable for water, and we put that in the box, too.

"What are we going to call this little rowdy?" my mother asked, watching the pup run around in the bottom of the box and fall into his water pan.

"Skipper," I said.

"You sound like you had that name picked out ahead of time."

"I've had it picked out *forever*," I admitted.

She kissed me. "Well, I know it's asking a lot, but you're already late for bed and tomorrow is a school day."

"Oh, Mom, if I could just stay up a *little* while—"

"Young man, whenever you want something special, you start talking like a Philadelphia lawyer. It won't work. Scoot!"

Reluctantly I obeyed. After all the lights were out and the vast country silence had slipped all through the house, Skipper began to whine in his box. I told myself that I was sparing my parents the noise, but in truth I had only been seeking an excuse. I went to the box and fumbled in the dark and found his wriggling, furry little body and took him out, carrying him back to bed with me. He cuddled against me and was immediately happy.

You're going to be the greatest dog in the world, Skipper, I thought. *You'll protect all of us and we'll run and play and I'll teach you to do tricks and obey me. And Bill Sheehan or anybody else will never bother me again. And it's going to be great!*

It was hours before I slept. I had never been so excited. I had no inkling of what lay ahead of us . . . Skipper and me.

4

Early in the morning I rigged up a little pen beside the house with some boards and chicken wire found in the barn and put Skipper inside it. He ran around aimlessly, sniffing the ground and bumping his nose against the boards. I petted him, put in his water pan, and gave him some leftover meat-loaf scraps and stale bread. He ignored the food and continued scurrying around. Reluctantly I left him and ran with Aggie to catch the bus.

The morning went well enough. Benny Harrison went back on the dunce stool again. Mrs. Broadus turned to him after recess and said, "Benny, I'm going to give you a chance to return to your chair. Did you study your lesson last night?"

"No," Benny sneered.

Mrs. Broadus was trying hard with him. "Well, I'll ask you a question anyway. If you can answer it, you can return to your regular seat. Now. Can you tell me who was President during the Civil War?"

Silence fell. She waited. Benny looked at her unblinkingly, his eyes slitted and cold.

"Well?" she prodded.

A smile quirked the corner of his mouth. "Mussolini?"

Mrs. Broadus jerked her head back, then raced to her big desk and pulled out her heavy yardstick. "All right, Benny! Hold out your hands."

He held them out. *Crack!* Down came the yardstick right across his outstretched knuckles. *Crack! Crack!* I flinched just seeing it. Benny Harrison's hands turned beet red. He did not quiver or change expression. Mrs. Broadus, breathing hard, stared at him. "*Now* will you behave?"

Benny just stared at her. She was defeated again. She stormed back to her desk.

I was in awe of him. God, he was tough.

As tough as he was, however, somehow he did not frighten me the way Bill Sheehan did. Of all the factions and groups within groups in our class of boys, Sheehan was the only one I instinctively recognized as truly and essentially evil. We all teased the girls, but he was the only one who pulled their hair really hard, or seemed to enjoy it the most if he saw hurt tears in their eyes. He was the only boy in our class I ever saw go out of his way to frighten or pick on a first-grader. Even Phil Inright and Jimmy Cantwell, the two biggest boys in the room, did not have that air of real viciousness about them. Sheehan was cruel and he was sneaky. And if he had not already picked me as a special target, I inadvertently assured his further attention that second day at lunch recess.

We were out on the playground, and the game of capture the flag was getting under way again. The fifth-graders, who far outnumbered us, had already gotten the flag out of our territory once, capturing two of our boys in the process. With Sheehan in the middle, we huddled up to plan our strategy.

"Okay, big shot," he said to me. "You bragged how fast you are. Let's see you go get the flag."

"By myself?" I asked.

"That's the way the game is played, kid."

"Well, wait," I said, sweating. "Maybe we ought to plan it out better."

"Like what?" Sheehan sneered, and all eyes were upon me.

"Well," I said, thinking fast, "maybe what we need is some strategy."

"Like what?" Sheehan repeated.

I raised my head from the huddle and looked across into enemy territory. A scheme formed in my mind. I ducked back down. "What if I run down around this end. Some of them will chase me. Then Jimmy starts in right here in the middle, going like mad. Then they're going to say, 'Hey! The first attack was a diversion, and the real attack is in the middle!' So they'll go for Jimmy."

"And you both get captured," Sheehan said.

"No, no! While we're both being chased, you and Phil are way down there at the far end, see? You've maybe already strolled across the line a few steps. You just keep sort of wandering along the edge of the field like you weren't in the game. Then when Jimmy and I are both getting caught, you and Phil run in from the trees down there at the far end and get the flag and get back with it!"

Sheehan's close-set eyes became sober. "We never tried anything like that."

"It will work!" Cantwell said excitedly. "It *will!*" Everybody in the huddle started jumping around, getting excited.

"Okay," Sheehan said grimly. "We'll try it."

We broke the huddle and ranged along the line. The fifth-graders faced us, scattered over the field. No strategy would have worked except that everyone in our grade didn't participate, and children from other rooms wandered freely over the area, so that the players were only a part of the human mosaic of the broad, grassy field. I walked south to the near end of the boundary, then turned and dashed into enemy territory. I wanted to be very sure everyone saw my intentions.

For a few seconds no one responded. Then there was a sharp cry and I saw a couple of fifth-graders running to cut me off. I pretended fear and scurried closer to the south boundary. They started to close. I turned on my speed and saw to my horror that they were speedier.

At this point there were other cries in the distance, and I turned a second to see Cantwell lumbering through the fifth-grade middle. Boys from near and far began to converge on him. Cantwell dodged one of them and fell, and just then a couple of fifth-graders tackled me.

Spitting dirt and grass, I was dragged back to the enemy rear. Cantwell was already there, along with a couple of other boys captured earlier. I looked up to see if Sheehan's main attack had gained the flag. Instead of a vacant branch, the flag waved brazenly in the wind. And coming at me, fifth-graders pinioning both his arms, was a muddy Sheehan. They shoved him into the capture circle.

"Goddam idiot!" he screamed at me. "Goddam moron! Goddam crumbum!"

"What happened?" I asked.

"They captured me, you queerbait! Nobody *ever* captured me before!"

I sighed. "Well, I guess it's no big deal."

Without warning, he hit me. There was a sharp flash of pain in my mouth as I sat down hard. Then I tasted blood and something—a tooth—almost went down my throat. Sheehan danced around me, thumbing his nose with his right fist and ducking his face in under his left shoulder. "Come on! Fight!"

I spat my tooth into the palm of my hand and looked at it. It was one from the side front that had been already loose, but nothing like this had ever happened to me before. I was dazed.

Sheehan kept dancing around and making snuffing noises as he thumbed his nose. "Come on! Come on! Fight! Come on!"

"I don't want to fight!" I protested. He looked absolutely stupid, but I was terrified.

"Aw, Bill," Cantwell said, "leave him alone. He didn't mean nothing."

"*You* want to fight?" Sheehan demanded, dancing around Cantwell. There was that crazy, cruel look in his eyes. "Come on, you fat slob!"

Distantly the lunch bell began ringing. Other boys who had ringed us began to break away and run for the building.

"Come on!" Sheehan taunted again, returning to me. "Coward!"

I sat in the wet grass, hating myself, unable to move.

"Aw, Bill," Cantwell said again.

Sheehan dropped his hands. Some of the mad glaze left his eyes as if some kind of spell had ended. He looked down at me with infinite disgust. "I'll finish you off later," he said, and ran for the building.

I got up shakily and brushed myself off. There was some blood on my shirt and hands. I got out my hankie and held it to my mouth as I limped toward the building. The playground had magically emptied. I entered via the south doors and went into the boys' room to try to clean myself up. Standing inside the door by one of the urinals, smoking a cigarette, was Benny Harrison.

"What happened to you, kid?" he demanded as I washed.

"Nothing," I muttered.

"Kid," he said heavily, "I asked you a question."

I swallowed and told him. As I did so, his hard face grew even harder. He tossed his cigarette butt into the toilet, flushed it, and walked out. When I got back to the classroom, he was already on the dunce stool, staring into his own private universe.

I said nothing, went to my seat, and joined the lesson. My mouth hurt but I had stopped the bleeding. I did not dare look at Sheehan. The arithmetic lesson flew by, and we did art. Then the bell rang for the short afternoon recess. I went to the bathroom and tried again to get the blood out of my shirt. When I left the room, the bell had already clanged to resume class. I went in and sat down. Benny Harrison, his face a little pink from exertion, came in right behind me. He perched on the stool. Mrs. Broadus closed the door. I noticed that Sheehan was not back.

A minute or two later he came in. He had a handkerchief to his face and the cloth was not sufficient to staunch the blood flowing freely from his nose. He had been crying and his face had tears and blood all over it. The room hushed.

"What happened to you?" Mrs. Broadus asked, shocked.

Sheehan's strained eyes darted behind the hankie. "I—fell down," he said, strangled.

There was a commotion. Mrs. Broadus took Sheehan to the

principal's office, and when he came back after a while the flow of blood had been stopped. His nose looked like one of those red rubber bulbs used by clowns. He sat very quietly through the last hour of school, blinking at his textbook.

After the final bell I did my best to avoid him, but it was impossible. As we all marched down the corridor toward the exits, teachers monitoring us, Sheehan managed to get next to me. The eyes he turned to me were bright with rage and hatred. "I'll get you," he said. "He can't protect you forever."

"*Why?*" I demanded despairingly. "I never did anything to you!"

Mrs. Broadus nudged me from behind with her yardstick. "No talking in line!"

"Remember," Sheehan whispered spitefully. "I'm gonna get you!"

We went onto the playground, split into lines to follow the school traffic guards to various streets. The lines loosened and we could talk now, and I looked around for Aggie and saw instead Benny Harrison.

He trotted up beside me, the gewgaws on his cap jingling. "What did he say to you just then, kid?"

"He said he'd get me."

Benny sighed. "Well, I guess you'll just have to fight him yet, then."

"Did you punch his nose during last recess?"

"Sure."

"Because he knocked my tooth out?"

"Sure."

"Why, Benny?"

"I dunno," Benny said. "I guess I like you, kid."

"*Why?*" I asked unbelievingly.

"I dunno," he repeated. He looked like he was casting around for a reason. "You got class. You're smarter than most of the guys in school. I seen that right away. And you're from Columbus. I dunno. I just like you. Don't worry about it. Maybe I'll change my mind."

We reached the street corner, waited for the guard to put the bamboo pole and flag across to block traffic, and crossed. I saw

Aggie hurrying along behind us and waited. Benny hesitated.

"You smoke, kid?" he asked.

"No," I told him.

"I didn't think so. See you." He turned and ran off.

At home, Skipper was ecstatic when I went up to his pen and started talking to him. I took him out and put him on the grass. He ran a few feet, then hunkered down and whined. I picked him up and examined him solicitously, but could find nothing wrong with his paws. The order of the day was to start on the garden plot, so I put a string around his neck and took him down to the weedy patch with me, tying him to the remains of the garden fence. The shovel and hoe were in the barn and I got them out, setting to work. It was a high and windy afternoon, weeds beginning to poke out of the dead leaves and underbrush of the plot. Getting the garden ready to plant was going to be a very big job.

Within a few minutes my mother left the house and came down the slope, the wind whipping her thin dress. She gave me a sunny, quizzical smile. "Hello, stranger."

"Hullo," I said, keeping my back partly to her.

"You didn't even come in and let me know when you got home."

"Well, I wanted to get started on this right away, Mom."

She walked closer and sharpened her tone. "I saw your shirt in the laundry. You changed and came right out here?"

"Yessum, I wanted to get started."

"What was that on your shirt?"

I turned to face her. She stared and then her eyes changed. "Your lip is all swollen!"

"I fell down," I lied. "I knocked out that loose baby tooth over here, see?" I stuck a finger in my mouth and gaped it for her.

"It must have *hurt!*" she said.

"Well, it was pretty loose."

She sighed. "You're all right?"

"Yessum."

"This is going to be an awfully big job, Danny, this garden."

"We'll get it, Mom. Don't worry about it."

"I know. But if your face hurts or anything, I don't want you out here today in this wind. We can work on it tomorrow."

"I'm fine. Really. And I've got Skipper to keep me company."

She turned to look at the puppy sitting forlornly on the end of his string leash. "He's going to be a big one, isn't he?"

"*Real* big," I said proudly.

She hesitated as if uncertain. "Well, I'll go back in. If your tooth starts bothering you, you just come in. All right?"

"All right, Mom."

She went back to the house. I dug for a while, my progress impeded by the fact that I couldn't stand on the shovel and make it go all the way in the way I had seen my father do it. When I stood on the shovel, it teetered and fell over with me. So I had to hack at the moist ground with the blade, then lift out small increments at a time.

"We'll make it, Skipper," I told my dog. He wagged his tail. "Get these weeds out and the top broken up, and then it'll rain and I can stand on the old shovel and it'll sink right in. Phew! If you were a little bigger maybe I could get *you* to help me dig."

I sat down, out of breath. Skipper whined. I crawled over to him and lay beside him in the wet, fragrant grass. He licked my hand as I petted him.

"You want to run around?" I asked. I untied the string.

Skipper ran a few paces, then hunkered down, whining.

"What's the matter with you, you old dummy?" I asked.

He turned and ran toward me. I held out my hand. He fell over it, scrambled, found it, began licking frantically. His tail going a mile a minute. Something about the way he had moved —the way he had *fallen over* my outstretched hand—linked in my mind with his behavior last night on the colonel's porch, his stumbling through his water pan. A cold hand gripped my midsection as I picked him up and held him up in front of me, staring into his brown eyes.

"Are you all right?" I asked softly.

He wriggled madly, trying to catch me with his pink, darting tongue. But the coldness was growing in me now and I held him fast, transferring his weight to my left hand. Freeing my right, I drew it back and made a sudden sharp gesture at him to make him flinch.

He did not flinch.

Heart pounding now, I put the puppy down. He sort of leaned against my feet, rubbing. I backed up sharply, leaving him alone in the grass. He hopped to his right and then to his left and then stopped, going to his round belly. He whined.

Creeping, I moved in front of him, knelt down not ten feet from him, held out my arms. He was panting. He seemed to stare right at me, and did not move.

"Skipper," I said.

With a little glad bound he jumped toward me and rolled into my lap, beside himself with joy. I picked him up again, holding him close to my face, looking into his eyes. They stared back, but now I knew with a sickening certainty that they stared but did not see.

Skipper was blind.

For a little while—I will never know how long—I squatted in the wet grass and held the pup. Sheer shock at first made thought impossible. I stroked his fur, felt his milk teeth gnaw nervously at my fingers, picked him up again and looked into his unseeing eyes to try to prove to myself that I was wrong. I wanted to cry, but the impact of this was beyond crying. It was the most terrible thing that had ever happened to me and I had nothing in my experience to help me cope with it.

There was no doubt. Skipper was blind.

I examined him repeatedly, hoping that somehow I was wrong. I made sharp gestures in front of his face and got no reaction whatsoever. A finger-snap made him blink or jump. All the while, he was wriggling happily, trying to lick my hands and face. He was perfect in every other way, and the most terrible thing was how *happy* he seemed. Evidently he had been born blind and knew no other condition.

My first logical reaction was anger at the colonel. He had done it on purpose, I thought. But then I realized this was crazy because *I* had been the one to pick Skipper from the litter, and had done so over the mild objections of both the colonel and my father. This was my own mistake, my own choosing of a puppy who could never live a normal life . . . if he lived a life at all.

For my next thought was of my father's reaction when he found out. He would either demand that we return Skipper to the colonel at once, or simply destroy him. The colonel's newspaper ad had not yet run; the other puppies were still available. I imagined us going back there, the colonel giving us another puppy in exchange. Then *he* would kill Skipper. Of that I had no doubt. I could practically hear him: *"Defective. Can't live. Blind dog is no good to anyone. I'll shoot him myself."*

The prospect filled me with horror and I hugged Skipper closer. "Don't worry," I crooned as he squirmed to lick my face. "They aren't going to hurt you, boy."

But how could I prevent it? I wasn't going to *keep* him—was I?

It was a possibility that I dreaded. My dream had been of a fine dog who would run and play with me, help me hunt rabbits, curl at the foot of my bed at night, go with me to school sometimes, perhaps, and just stand there, watching Bill Sheehan, so that Sheehan would know he must never touch a hair of my head again. What good was a blind puppy to me?

With a burst of angry resentment I tossed Skipper to the ground. He hit awkwardly, yelping with pain, and rolled over. Then he took a few meaningless steps and went to his belly, in the gesture of total lostness that now made perfect sense to me. He whined.

"Oh, you dummy," I murmured, hurrying to pick him up again and send him into fresh spasms of joy.

No, Skipper could not be returned to the colonel. If I could possibly keep his blindness a secret just until Friday, I thought, then the other puppies would be adopted and that possibility was foreclosed. But what, then, of my father?

I saw what I had to do. I had to fool everyone, my mother and father and Aggie, until Friday at the earliest. Then the colonel's other pups would be gone. After that, I could pretend great shock when one of my family noticed Skipper's blindness. Maybe—*maybe*—they would have mercy on him.

It seemed the best plan I could come up with. But then a danger occurred to me. If I admitted the problem now, there would be a new puppy, a whole one . . . the one I had always dreamed about. But if I waited and deceived everyone, the other pups would be gone. Then I might very well lose Skipper —and with him all my chances of having any dog at all for perhaps a long, long time.

It stopped me momentarily. I looked at Skipper again. He was such a fat little mutt. Holding him close, I could have sworn he was grinning at me.

"I ought to let you go," I told him softly. "If I try to save your worthless life, I might lose *everything*. I ought to play it safe."

His pink tongue darted out and caught my nose.

"Quit that!" I groaned. "Stop it! Oh, Skipper, that's not fair! You don't play fair at all, do you? Stop!"

He would not. He lathered my face, sheer joy. I hugged him closer. The decision was made.

5

The German prisoners began arriving the next day, and my father was scarcely home at all through the weekend as more trainloads came in. Something had gone wrong somewhere, and instead of a couple of hundred, as anticipated, there were by Sunday afternoon almost four hundred captured German soldiers in the camp. My father went night and day, making new arrangements. New construction was necessary, he said, and some of the prisoners would temporarily sleep in tents. More guards were needed, more kitchen help, more maintenance people, more food, more platters and utensils, more bedding, more everything. The colonel had sent off many frantic telegrams to his superiors in Washington, and some bedding and supplies had come promptly from Columbus' Fort Hayes. His request for additional military personnel, my father said, had been turned down flatly with instructions to "recruit additional civilian labor as feasible." Which threw it directly into my father's lap.

The town of Harmony was stirred up. My father took enough time off Saturday afternoon to take us into the grocery, and it seemed every business and home had an American flag flying in front of it. The weekly paper—the one with the colonel's ad in it—had featured news of the prisoners' arrival and an editorial pleading for calm and cooperation with camp officials. My father said some merchants—those in line to make big sales to the camp—backed the installation. Everyone else, he said, was either flatly against or simply scared. I saw one sign reading, TAKE THEM TO FT. KNOX.

"They wouldn't be so excited if they could see a lot of those poor devils," my father said. "We're going to have to have a daily shuttle to Fort Hayes for medical treatments if they don't assign some real doctors down here permanently."

"Have the prisoners been mistreated?" my mother asked sharply.

"No. Not really. But they've been through a *war,* Elizabeth. From what I've heard so far, a lot of them were having a pretty tough time of it with their own units before they got swept up and captured. Some of them have suffered minor wounds . . . some are just out of hospitals for things more serious. Then they've been herded from place to place, trucked, railroaded . . . they're a million miles from home, malnourished, a lot of them, not sure what's going to be done to them, no money, no cigarettes, nothing."

"Well, you're going to treat them well, aren't you?"

"Of course." My father's forehead creased. "The colonel didn't help their spirits any, though, when he had them stand formation this morning."

"What did he tell them?"

"Read them the riot act. Ran off a long list of things a man could be put into solitary confinement for, explained that the guards all have live ammunition, told the German officers to organize their men into the work details as they saw fit, but any malingering in the fields would be blamed on the officers as well as the soldiers caught at it." My father sighed. "It was rough."

My mother watched him. "Too rough?"

"Too rough."

"Did you say so?"

"Of course not. You've met the colonel. What would he have told me? That I'm a civilian subject to military authority. That I'm expendable."

"He wouldn't *dare* say that!"

My father's smile had no pleasure in it. "Never mind. Things will work out. I've visited with some of the prisoners already. A surprising number of them speak some English. They don't want trouble any more than I do."

We had pulled into the grocery store parking lot. My mother paused before getting out. "They have to be treated right, George."

"I know that. They will be."

She looked at him another few seconds, then seemed satisfied. "You're going to do the other shopping while I start in here?"

"Yes." My father reached for his wallet.

"The grocery money will stretch," she told him.

"No. I want something else." He took out a bill and handed it out the car window to her. "Maybe you could get four extra cartons of cigarettes."

"Four! I'll be lucky to find any!"

"They've had plenty here lately. Get them if they have them."

"People will think we're hoarders."

"Let them think what they want."

"What on *earth* are you going to do with that many cigarettes?"

My father looked at her, his smile crooked, as it was when he was embarrassed.

"Oh," my mother said.

"Well, I thought a few of them might get a smoke, anyway."

"You'd give a smoke to a *German?*" I burst out, shocked.

"Squirt, I've told you. They're people. Just like us."

"Not like us," I said indignantly. "*We* didn't run over France!"

"Son, there are rules. If you're a part of civilization, you obey them."

"We've got to be tough," I countered stoutly. "You start letting people push you around and there's just no *end* to it."

"You think it's being pushed around," he asked quietly, "to give them a smoke?"

"It might be! It might be!"

He sighed. "Treating someone with decency is not a sign of weakness."

"You give any sign you might be weak," I said, "and they're liable to just run right over you." I was dimly aware that we might be talking about different things entirely now. He was talking about the prisoners, and God knows I was fervently trying to feel nothing but hate for them, as was my duty as an American citizen as I saw it. But at the same time I had this mental picture, and it was of Bill Sheehan thumbing his nose combatively and dancing around me while I cowered. Being tough with the Germans was suddenly all mixed up with my own desperate need to defeat my fear of Sheehan. "You got to be *tough,* Dad."

"Well, I'll just be tough in my way, and you be tough in yours. Okay?"

My mother seemed to think it was time to step in. "Are you going to the hardware store now?"

"Yes. I'll get the towel racks for the bathroom and the new fixture for the kitchen."

"Get chrome. If they have chrome—"

"I doubt I'll find any chrome. But I'll get the best we can afford."

She accepted this. "Are you going to have time to get Danny by the shoe store too?"

"We'll go there first," my father said, and put the car in reverse to back out.

A trip to the shoe store was always a big event, and despite my worry about Skipper I had given the matter of new shoes considerable thought. My brown oxfords were through on the right sole and almost through on the left. When my mother took me for clothing, she picked it out and let me bless her decision. With my father it was different, and as we entered the shoe store I saw what I wanted immediately: a pair of very dark lace-up boots like those Benny Harrison wore.

"Those," I said as soon as the clerk had measured my foot and had me stick it under the fluoroscope machine.

"*Those?*" my father repeated incredulously as the old man brought the boots.

"They'll be real practical," I said. "I can work in them and wear them to school both."

My father looked at them. They were easily as ugly as Benny Harrison's, with thick black soles and heels, lacing from the toe all the way to the knee, and a flapped pocket on the side where a man could carry a knife. "These weigh a ton. Sure you don't want tennis shoes?"

"Well, Dad, I've got last year's tennis shoes and they're still good. This will give me an extra pair."

"Your mother would never let you wear these to church. You'd have to polish up these old ones for church."

"Okay!"

"How much are these?" my father asked, hefting the boots.

"Four-eighty, sir," the old man said. "We're clearing them out."

I waited in agony. My father sighed. "Try them on."

I tried them. They were stiff and heavy, and they hurt my feet. I said I would wear them. I clomped out feeling tougher already, and tried walking like Benny did.

My mother took one look and had a fit. But a sale was a sale. When we got home, I dug around in my junk and found an old beanie a little like Benny's. Hunting up some buttons, a wheel off a model, and a Roosevelt button, I got busy sewing. The hat did not turn out as well as Benny's, but by the time it was finished I was proud of it. After my father hurried back to the camp that evening, I felt it safe to take Skipper for a walk. I wore the new boots to help break them in, but after we walked a few hundred yards down the slope toward the fence separating our little place from the big farm behind us, I stopped and went barefooted. The boots had already raised four or five raw red blisters.

My greatest concern through that weekend, however, was Skipper. I could not keep him in the box in the room. But every time I let him out, I knew his condition would be noticed instantly. It was agony, I think, for him as well as for me.

That afternoon when I let him out of the box to change the papers in it, he did not go to his belly and whine as he had on earlier occasions. He sallied across the room, tail wagging. And walked right into the leg of my desk. The blow staggered him and he fell sideways, fat little legs sprawling. He got up and walked into the wall. Sitting up, shaking his head, he looked pitifully into his own private darkness and wet on the floor.

I carried him outside in my arms so no one would notice that he couldn't navigate. Taking him out beyond the patch that was going to be our garden, I put him down in some ankle-high grass. He sniffed the grass with intense interest and wandered a few feet away from my feet.

"You'll learn, boy," I told him encouragingly. "You've got a great nose, right? And you can learn sounds, too. Like I'm teaching you my voice right now, right?"

He moved a little farther from me, and then lay down and rolled over and over in the damp grass, playing and biting at his own tail, which he could not quite reach. He made little snapping sounds with his milk teeth. I laughed and watched, and then fell silent.

He got up and stood very still, one floppy ear cocked. He took a few steps tentatively, moving in a blind half circle. I remained silent, driven by some urge to experiment. He stood still. He began whining. He was less than ten feet from me, but he was hopelessly lost.

"Here I am, Skipper," I said, patting my hands together.

His tail began a mile a minute. He started off in the direction away from me. I hurried over and scooped him up. He went wild with pleasure, wriggling, licking my face, biting at my nose and ears. I hugged him tightly. "You'll be fine!" I told him. But *how?*

A start had to be made. Carrying Skipper to the little building that served as a barn, I looked around at rusty bits of metal and broken tools left by some former occupant. Hanging from a nail bearded with rust was a thin length of leather. It had a serviceable strap fastener on one end. I sawed through it with my pocketknife, measured it around Skipper's neck, and pushed in a couple of fastener holes. I put it on him and it made a usable collar.

There was also string and twine in the barn. Finding a three-foot piece that seemed stout, I tied one end to the collar and held the free end in my hand, forming a leash.

"Okay, boy," I said. "Let's practice."

Skipper walked to the end of the makeshift leash and pulled himself over backward. I tugged him onto his feet again. Pulling, I managed to get him to walk in a crooked line out of the barn and into the sunlight. There was a rotting barrel beside the door.

"Look out—!" I started.

Too late. He walked into the barrel.

For a moment I felt utter despair. There was no chance. He was completely helpless. He could be lost a few feet from me, and even with a leash, every obstacle became an impossible hazard. How could I ever do it?

Even as I thought this, however, he was scurrying around blindly, sniffing. He encountered one of my feet. His tail began pumping gladly. He yipped with glee and rolled over, trying to play with my shoe. I gave up on my despair. There had to be a way. There *had to*.

I had been planning further exploration of the drainage pipe into the creek and had gotten new batteries for my Cub Scout flashlight, the only souvenir I had from my abortive time in the Cubs except for one badly braided whistle strap. Now I felt a need to do something to take my mind off Skipper, and the afternoon loomed vacantly. Getting the flashlight and a ball of kite twine, I avoided detection by my mother or Aggie and set off alone.

Fresh greenery concealed many of the stickers in the raspberries, and I encountered them painfully again on the way. I tried to take a more direct route through the woods to the area where I remembered the pipe, but it was all what we called

brier patch in that direction, and I had to return. Getting to the
creek in much the same place I had visited it before, I scrambled down the steep bank, falling one foot into the water again,
and proceeded to my left. Rain had raised the water level temporarily, bringing down all sorts of new and interesting debris,
including a soggy orange crate, some beer bottles, and two old
tires. I inspected the tires, hoping to find a red inner tube for a
rubber gun. I was disappointed.

Going on, I almost had to search for the pipe. New spring
weeds had sprouted all around it, virtually hiding it from view.
If I had not known the pipe was there, I might have missed it,
because no water happened to be draining from it this day.

Climbing up inside with confidence, I was again struck by the
cold, dank odor from the bowels of the earth. I decided possibly it was too late in the day for a major expedition, or that I
should have brought sandwiches. Then, recognizing this as cowardly rationalization, I braced myself and switched on my
small flashlight. It penetrated about a dozen paces into the
gloom, its shaft visible in wafting strands of some horrible
whitish gas. Maybe I needed a gas mask and should wait. But
then I recognized *that* as an excuse, too.

I tied one end of my kite string to one of the bushes that
partly obscured the pipe opening. Then, unwinding string with
my left hand while I held the flashlight with my right, I started
inside.

Things went well for the first few minutes. I moved along
steadily, unwinding string, the flashlight now my only illumi-
nation in a world of utter blackness. I had gotten used to the
gassy odor, but I was sweating despite the low temperature. I
could not get out of my mind the idea that I could (a) get lost,
(b) be buried by a cave-in, (c) get caught in some flash flood,
a mammoth toilet-flushing from wherever this thing originated,
or (d) meet some kind of hideous creature. I tried not to think
but just keep hunching along.

After a while I paused to rest, and looked behind me. The
opening was *far* behind me—a pinprick hole of brilliant sunlight. I sat catching my breath, looking back at the bit of light. I
felt like an outcast from the real world, and began growing sen-

timental about sunlight and living things while I, here, was doomed to the life of a mole. *Mole Man!* It sounded like a great idea for a comic strip. To get the feel of the idea better, testing the milieu, I switched off my flashlight—felt the darkness close around me—and got it back on quickly.

To go on or not go on? It was really starting to get late, I told myself, and I ought to work in the garden. Also there was the pressing matter of installing the rubber bands in my model Spad. I imagined my mother, weeping and wringing her hands. *Where, oh, where, has my darling boy gone?* Possibly I owed it to her—

But again I saw where my wishful thinking was taking me, and set my teeth and pressed on, laying out more string behind me.

Another hundred paces up the tunnel, it began to bend to my right. The bend was slow but definite. Sweat dripped off my nose and into the corners of my mouth despite the dank cool. I told myself I would keep going and see where this baby *went*. I glanced back and could no longer see any trace of the outside world. I was feeling homesick for it. I gritted my teeth and kept going, my aching feet in the hard leather boots the only sound.

Up ahead, then, however, I thought I heard something. I froze, holding my breath. It was vague—a *rumbling*. I could not make it out. It did not sound like running water or wind. It was a sound of some kind of movement . . . a great, vast, *horrible* movement.

Go ahead! Go find out what it is!

"Are you crazy? Do you want to get killed?" I asked aloud.

But I knew I was close to whatever answer this riddle must have. The vast sounds ahead were not as far as I had already come. My legs ached and I was almost out of string. I had come a very long way.

"You might as well go ahead," I told myself softly. "If you don't, you're just going to hate yourself. And you'll just have to come back all this way another time. You know you won't be satisfied till you *know*."

I wished I knew what time it was. Maybe there really wasn't time.

I inched another few paces forward.

The flashlight tremored and went yellow in my hand, almost going out.

Thought vanished. The next thing I knew, I was running for my life. I didn't stop until I had reached the sun-flooded mouth of the tunnel and tumbled out onto the wet dirt, gasping for breath.

After I regained my composure, I looked back up at the pipe. It certainly did not look frightening from *here*. I shook my head, groaning.

"Now you've got to do it *again!*" I told myself disgustedly.

But not today.

On Monday, true to my plan, I wore my new boots and took my beanie in my lunch pail with the baloney sandwich, milk, and banana. Once Aggie was in her classroom, I got the beanie out and put it on. Jimmy Cantwell met me in the hall just as I did it.

"Who do *you* think you are?" Cantwell demanded.

I gave him my slit-eyed Benny Harrison tough look. "Who's askin'?"

Cantwell punched me in the stomach and waltzed into the classroom.

The bell rang. Still gasping for breath, I staggered in after him. Most students were at the desks, and Mrs. Broadus was writing something on the blackboard, but she glanced over and saw me. Her expression went fierce and she came across the room at me like a Sherman tank. With one swooping gesture she knocked my beanie off my head and propelled me toward the dunce stool. "What do you think you're doing, coming to school looking like that?" she demanded. "Get up there! You want a hat? You'll get a hat!" She crammed the dunce cap on my skull with force that almost unseated me.

At first recess, Cantwell punched me again and Phil Inright shoved me down. Fighting tears, I got up and shuffled toward the building. Benny Harrison was standing there watching. I

must have given him a wildly accusing look, asking silently why
he had suddenly stopped championing me.

"Kid," he said, "it comes with the territory. You wear the
uniform, you better be prepared to fight."

At the end of the day Mrs. Broadus did not return my beanie
and I did not ask for it. Once home, I removed the boots, sur-
veyed the raw blisters, and got out my old tennis shoes. They
were too small this year. I put them on anyway.

For another day or two my secret about Skipper remained
secure. I worked in the garden and began to get a large portion
of it weeded and broken a few inches deep. I kept Skipper close
beside me at all times, and everyone else was so busy with
other things that he passed casual muster. My father continued
long hours at the camp, my mother was now making new curtains, and Aggie was hysterical with her kittens. I had no idea
what I would do when someone noticed, but each day that
passed gave me a false sense of new security.

It was either that Wednesday or Thursday afternoon that I
was still working at the back of the garden plot, Skipper tied
nearby. In the fields of the big farm behind our place, the German prisoners had been at work for two days. It had been exciting at first to see the trucks thrum down the road and the
prisoners being unloaded, a handful of soldier guards watching,
the prisoners in dark fatigues and caps, carrying shovels, hoes,
and rakes. But the prisoners worked routinely, breaking rows in
the distance, and there was no incident. Already, working the
garden, I was paying little or no attention to the workers across
the fence until suddenly I became aware that someone was
watching me.

I looked up and saw a tall, slender man in the prisoner fatigues standing not far away. A second prisoner was a few
paces behind him, and a soldier with a rifle brought up the rear.
The nearest prisoner had buckets in his hands. He had close-
cropped hair, a rather large nose, and a crooked smile. He was
perhaps my father's age.

"We were told we could get water," he said in a thick accent.

I scrambled back, looking around for a rock or stick. "Get away from me!"

He stopped, eyes drooping. "What is it?"

"Stay away! I'll yell! My dad is important! You try anything and you'll be sorry!"

The second prisoner came up beside this first one. He was younger. Shockingly, he looked not all that much older than I. He had a poor complexion, pimples, and he looked so skinny and sad in his oversized fatigues that I felt sorry for him. Then I thought, *You can't feel sorry for these guys! They're the enemy!*

The first German was watching me closely, with a grave, kind expression. "There is nothing to fear, young man."

"*I* know you guys!" I replied defensively.

"We have met?" He looked surprised.

"I mean I know who you are. You're Germans."

The older man exchanged glances with the boy beside him. "He is perceptive." They both smiled.

It made me mad. I caught Skipper's leash and started pulling him away. He hopped after me and ran into a fence post, staggering himself.

The older German registered dismay. "The puppy. He is blind?"

"What's it to you?" I shot back.

"Poor puppy," he said softly, coming over and bending to pet Skipper, who of course went crazy with pleasure and relief, licking his hands and rolling over. The German chuckled and held his head to look into his eyes. "Yes. Blind. What a pity."

"He can be trained," I snapped.

"Of course he can," the German answered as if that were obvious.

I was stunned. "He *can?* Really?"

"Of course. I had a dog just like this one."

I forgot to hate him. "Like *Skipper?*"

"*Ja.* Heidi. She was a very good dog. But blind. Like this one."

"How long . . . did she live?"

"Heidi? A blind dog with no other faults can have a fine, long life."

"How long *did* she live?" It was terribly important.

The soldier strode up. "Hey, kid, can we draw some water?"

"Right over there," I told him, and returned my gaze to the German. "How long did she live?"

His smile was sad. "She may still be alive . . . if the bombers have not struck my home near Munich."

"You mean she didn't die from being blind?" I asked excitedly.

"No. I am a trainer of dogs . . . a . . . veterinarian." He raised his eyebrows. "*Was* a veterinarian. Heidi . . . there are ways to train such a dog. It is hard. It can be done. Your dog, if he lives, will always require special care. But such a dog can be trained, have a good life."

"How do you train him?" I demanded. "What do you do first?"

"Come on!" the soldier said sharply.

The German flinched and started to turn away with the buckets.

"What do I do first?" I called after him.

He glanced back. "Teach him always to come to the sound of your voice. Teach him to walk the leash close to your side."

"Come on, come on!" the soldier said.

I sat in the garden and watched them go to the old well, pump it, finally get water coursing up out of the earth, fill the buckets. I was excited beyond belief. Unless he had lied to me—and he did not seem a liar—I had new hope.

As they started back across the yard toward me, I saw that my German limped rather badly, spilling some of the water. His face was intent on his task as if it was difficult for him. On impulse I left the garden and intercepted him. "What's your name?" I asked, and then, seeing that might sound impolite, added, "I'm Danny Davidson."

He looked down at me, his heavily lined face breaking into another smile. He put down his buckets, extended his hand. "I am Rudi Gerhardt. I am pleased to make your acquaintance."

The soldier, who had hung back getting a drink of his own,

hurried over. "I'm not telling you again, Gerhardt! Move it!"

"And you really had a blind dog like Skipper?" I asked him.

Rudi Gerhardt picked up his buckets again. "Yes. I would like to talk to you about it, but you see we must hurry now. Perhaps there will be another day."

"And maybe you can tell me more about training Skipper!"

"If there is a way we can have time, of course."

He walked away then, skirting the garden and going downhill to the little creek, crossing it with his fellow prisoner and the soldier, limping out into the field. I saw the men gather and the ladle with water passed. It seemed a very great moment. I had met my first German prisoner, and suddenly everything about Skipper's future looked brighter.

I raced back to the garden and sat down with the pup. Taking the string leash in hand, I tugged on it gently. "Skipper," I said firmly, "here." I tugged again. He came to me. The training had begun. I was not going to give up easily now . . . even if it meant collaboration with one of the enemy.

6

For supper that night we had our first real guests. My mother flurried through the house most of the afternoon, brushing at imaginary specks of dirt between trips to the kitchen where a pot roast produced an indescribably lovely aroma. My father came home a little after six, quite early for him, and immediately went to the bedroom, returning in a fresh white shirt and different bow tie. Following orders, I took a bath, splashing the water in the tub a lot to make it sound like I was doing an exceptionally good job, and then put on my school clothes. By six-forty, the table was set with linen and our good china, and Aggie was sitting in the living room, swinging her legs, dressed in her best pink pinafore, white hose, and sandals. No one had bothered to tell Aggie and me the names of the guests.

At about ten minutes before seven, a car sounded in the front. My father put down the newspaper and went to the window. "They're here," he called toward the kitchen, and my mother came out, removing her apron.

I went to peer out too. I saw a rotund man in a dark suit, a small woman with gray hair, and Bill Sheehan coming across the yard from a black Cadillac sedan.

"What's *he* doing here?" I gasped.

"Who?" my father replied. "Oh. You mean the boy? You ought to know him, Danny. He's in your grade at school, isn't he?"

"I know him," I said, strangled.

"Let's all be on our best behavior," my mother said. "The Sheehans are very nice people. We want to be friends with them. That's why they're here."

There was a rap on the door, my father opened it, and the family came in. During a confusion of hearty greetings, Bill and I glared at each other. He was wearing Sunday clothes and looked more uncomfortable than I felt. Everyone sat down: my mother and Mrs. Sheehan on the couch, my father on a straight chair, Mr. Sheehan in his favorite chair, Aggie on the floor, Bill on a straight chair, me on the window sill across the room from him.

"Hot," Mr. Sheehan said, mopping his prodigious forehead. "You folks are lucky, though. It's closer in town. Nice place you have here."

"We're just getting it fixed up," my mother told him.

Sheehan rolled his eyes around. "Well, that's obvious, but you've made a lot of progress. I know how long the house was abandoned. My bank owns the mortgage with the owner, you know."

"I didn't know that," my father said, smiling as if it were amusing.

"Oh yes," Sheehan said. "Of course, Farmers and Citizens owns most of the mortgages in these parts. You ever decide to buy, I'm sure we'll be doing some business."

"Well, we might think about that one day."

Mrs. Sheehan chirped, "It will be a very nice area again, I'm sure, once those Germans are gone."

"The camp is miles from here," my father told her. "And there isn't really any danger."

"No danger! How can you say there's no danger? All those Nazis just waiting for a chance to escape and plunder?"

"Now, Effie," Sheehan said indulgently. He looked at my father. "I've explained repeatedly that the camp means real financial help for Harmony and its environs. We all know you people are doing everything in your power to make the camp secure, and . . . well, for the sake of business, you aren't going to hear any of us speaking publicly against it."

Mrs. Sheehan shuddered. "It makes me nervous being even this close." She looked at my mother. "How do you *stand* it, my dear?"

"Stand it?" my mother repeated slowly. "Well, it's different, after living all my life in the city, but it's beautiful. I think we're going to get used to it and—"

"No, no! I mean being so close to all those rapacious prisoners?"

"Well, I'm sure there's probably some danger. But I don't think there's much. They're under guard. And if they escaped, where would they escape *to?* I think they're probably glad to be safe where they are."

"That's the ticket!" Sheehan said. "Exactly the right line for public consumption! Good!" He winked at my father. "Excellent, George! Between us, we'll get through this crisis in fine shape, eh?"

My father's forehead wrinkled. "Crisis? There really isn't any crisis. We don't expect any trouble."

"Just keep the guns ready, eh? Crackerjack!"

My mother stood. "Excuse me. I have to see to things in the kitchen."

"I'll help, dear," Mrs. Sheehan said, and followed her. Their voices echoed from the kitchen.

Sheehan glanced their way, then leaned his ponderous weight closer to my father, lowering his voice. "I sympathize, George. Keeping a woman happy in the danger zone this way. Believe me, it's a patriotic thing to do. Anything any of us can do to help, don't hesitate. All of us must do our share." He turned to me without pause. "And when your dad is off at work and you're home, you keep a sharp eye out, eh? Know where all the guns are? Good. If any of those bastards ever start coming toward the house, don't hesitate. Stack them up like cordwood!"

"Those prisoners aren't going to try to escape!" my father said. "I meant it when I said that!"

"We'll hope you're right, George. But it doesn't hurt to be ready. Believe me, it doesn't hurt to be ready—and it doesn't hurt for those Germans to *know* we're ready. I can speak from experience, talking to many in town. Those Germans might think we're yokels, but I know different. Harmony is an armed camp. There's a loaded gun near every doorway. If they *do* try anything, you won't have to rally your guards. All you'll have to do is send the hearse."

My father's face was pale and strained. "None of that is going to happen."

"I hope not. I indeed hope not. But when you talk to those Germans, it will never hurt to remind them that we're all good Americans here. There are no sympathizers. Even the old German families are loyal. We've checked them out very, very carefully. No one will help those people if they try anything. There are a lot of us just *aching* for a chance to strike a blow for freedom—and reduce the cost to the taxpayers out there at the same time." Sheehan grinned a wolfish grin. "You understand?"

"Yes," my father said huskily. "But—"

Sheehan turned to me. "I understand you and Bill are good pals at school. Is that right?"

I hesitated an instant. "Yes, sir," I said.

"Good," the big man said.

Why, I wondered, had I agreed with him? My impulse had been to blurt out that he was crazy. I glanced from him to Bill, who sat watching me with a hint of his father's wolfish grin, and then to my father. He looked puzzled and worried and sad. Why had *either* of us allowed this man to say outrageous things, I wondered.

My mother came in to announce the meal was ready. We all went to the table and began passing dishes. In addition to the roast there were, of course, potatoes and carrots, green beans, a salad, fresh-baked bread, milk for us and coffee for them. It was a delicious feast. I tried to use my best table manners and took secret pleasure in seeing Bill chew with his mouth open.

Mr. Sheehan shoveled the food in fast, asking for seconds and then thirds. He sweated heavily, wiping his forehead often with a damp handkerchief. Most of the conversation was his. He told a long story about the Chamber of Commerce and plans for the Fourth of July, and then explained how activities at the country club had been curtailed to save supplies and contribute to the war effort. He seemed to be making a serious effort not to talk about the camp. Everything he talked about instead reeked of money.

"Just remember," he said at one point, "there's a silver lining to everything. This war is a terrible thing, but we're going to win it. And after the war there's going to be a boom like none this country ever saw. Harmony is going to be in the middle of it, George. There's going to be an enormous amount of money to be made. You're lucky to be here, making good friends, getting in on the ground floor."

My father smiled faintly. "I'm not averse to making some money."

"And you will," Sheehan said. "Believe me, you will. People already like you. You're doing a fine, necessary job. We take care of our own. For men like you the sky will be the limit!"

After the meal, which was topped by apple pie, the women went to the kitchen to stack the dishes. Aggie tagged along, jabbering. My father and Mr. Sheehan went into the living room, where my father tapped his cigarette and lit it while Sheehan took out a large dark cigar and began puffing it contentedly. My father suggested I show Bill my room. I had no choice. The two of us went down the hall and into my room, where I flicked on the lights.

Sheehan looked around at the desk, the bed, the models on strings. "Your models, huh?"

"Yes."

He reached up and flipped one of them contemptuously, making it gyrate on its string. "All dime models."

"I've made some fifty-cent models," I lied.

"Yeah? Where are they, then?"

"I gave them to relatives in Columbus."

"Yeah, I'll just bet you did."

Before I could reply, Skipper made a noise with his thumping tail in the carton partly hid behind the bed.

"What's that?" Sheehan asked, walking over. "Hey. A mutt."

"Be careful," I said quickly. "He's little."

Sheehan reached down and picked Skipper out of the box. Skipper frantically licked at his face. "Yuk!" Sheehan put him on the floor. Skipper dashed across the room and banged head-long into a leg of the desk, rattling it. He yelped in pain. I hurried to pick him up.

"What the hell's wrong with that dog?" Sheehan asked. "Did you see him run into that desk?"

"He's fine," I said, holding Skipper close.

"Lemme see," Sheehan said.

"No!"

He tugged at Skipper. "I'll just look, for cripe's sake." I had to let Skipper go or he might have been hurt. Sheehan held him up in front of him and looked into his eyes. "Well, I'll be!" he said softly.

"It's the bright light," I said. "It was dark and—"

Sheehan put Skipper on the floor. Skipper took a few steps and hunkered down, whining. Sheehan went over to him and made a sharp movement as if to kick him. Skipper did not react at all.

Sheehan looked up at me, surprise in his pale, cruel eyes. "Do you know this mutt is—"

"I know," I said. "But nobody else does. I'm going to try to train him."

"You can't train no—"

"I *can!* I *will!* A—somebody told me you could."

Sheehan stared at me a moment, then started for the door.

"No one else knows!" I whispered. "Bill! Please don't tell anybody! *Please!* All I need is a few days to start getting him trained."

Sheehan stared back at me. "Kid, you're nuts."

"Please, Bill. Please!"

He hurried out into the hall. A moment later I heard his

voice loud in the living room. "Dad! Come and see! Danny's got a mutt and it's blind as a bat!"

It was much later, and I was alone in my room, when my father tapped gently on the door. I was sitting on the side of my bed in my underwear, holding Skipper. When the door opened, a shaft of light fell across both of us. My father's tall shadow moved. "Son?"

"Yessir?"

He came in and sat beside me on the bed. He didn't speak and neither did I. I knew Aggie had gone to bed and my mother was still in the kitchen doing dishes. I was crushed by humiliation and fear.

The scene had been far worse than I could have imagined it. My father and Mr. Sheehan had come into the bedroom at once after Bill summoned them. My father's examination of Skipper only proved to him what I already knew. He looked at me in shocked disbelief.

"A shame," Mr. Sheehan rumbled. "Have to be put to sleep, of course."

"No!" I screamed angrily, forgetting all politeness.

"No choice," Sheehan told my father as if I weren't there. "Better to do it quickly before too much attachment can form."

"We'll have to think about it," my father had said. "Maybe it can be fixed."

The discussion went on and on. Sheehan did not think blindness in a dog could be repaired. I said I could train Skipper. My father said he had never heard of that. Sheehan said dogs could be put to sleep with no pain. My father got that sad look of perplexity he sometimes got when dealing with me, and said we would discuss it later. We all went back into the living room where I squirmed for more than another hour, Bill giving me smirking looks. When they finally left, I fled back to my room. Then for a while I had heard my mother and father talking quietly alone.

"He *knew* it?" my mother said more loudly at one point.

Later: "Oh, George, I don't see *how*—"

Aggie knew, too. She tiptoed past my door later. The house

got more quiet. I thought about Bill Sheehan and wished I was like Robin or the Submariner or the Green Lantern . . . and *then* what I would do to him for this. But mostly I just held Skipper, feeling his intense body heat. *They can't kill you. They can't. You're mine. I love you.*

Now, finally, my father spoke in the dimness. "You knew, Squirt?"

"Yes."

"Since when?"

"The other day."

"How did you find out?"

"He bumped into something, or something."

My father sighed. "When did you plan to tell the rest of us?"

"I dunno. After I had him trained."

"Trained?"

"To stay on a leash, come to me when I call, stay put when I tell him to."

"Son, think about Skipper. If he could think, do you think he really would want that? He can't *see*. He'll never know what you look like. He'll never be able to see the sky or chase a rabbit or run in the woods. He's crippled. Do you think he would want to stay alive like that?"

"I know if I was blind I wouldn't like it—I would hate it awful—but I would still want to try to stay alive."

"Dogs aren't like people."

"He likes to eat. He likes me to hold him. He loves me. He's growing. He had a mom and dad. He doesn't want to *die*."

My father took a slow, deep breath. "If you let him go now, it will hurt for a while. It will hurt to beat the band. I know that. But you haven't had him long. You'll get over it. You can have another dog—"

"I don't *want* another dog! I want Skipper!"

"My point, Squirt, is that the longer you keep him, the harder it will be to let him go."

"Why do I have to let him go at all? I can train him! He'll be good. I won't let him be a nuisance."

"Honey," he said despairingly, "it's not us I'm worried

about. It's *you*. Don't you see you're just asking us to let you open yourself up to all kinds of heartache?"

"I don't care! I want him!"

"You've got your school work. You're going to have to help a lot around the house . . . in the yard and garden. Then when you do have some time off, wouldn't you rather go down to the creek, fishing? Or swimming? Or work on your models? You don't know what you're letting yourself in for."

"I don't care! I don't care!"

"Squirt," he said heavily after a pause, "you're just not old enough to make this decision. It's going to have to be made for you."

I began to cry.

"Life," he went on slowly as I wept, trying to stifle my sobs, "is full of disappointments, Squirt. You know, the one thing a father and mother would like to do is keep their children from those disappointments. But they're there . . . it's the way it always is. Maybe . . . becoming a man . . . is all disappointments. You try so hard . . . you want to be a man . . . get ahead . . . take care of your family . . . and things don't always go right. Life isn't all joy. You . . . start out scared . . . you end up scared . . ."

"You?" I choked. "Scared?"

He put a hand on my shoulder. "Of course."

"What were *you* ever scared of?"

"Of not being smart enough. Of not getting ahead. Of not being able to take care of your mother and you kids. Of changing . . . or staying put. Of not being liked. Of being weak, or stupid, or useless. Of failure." He gently squeezed my neck. "Most people, Squirt, are scared more than half the time."

"But you're great," I told him. "You always know everything, and I don't know nothing. I'm just *dumb*."

"Hey, you're not dumb."

"I'm dumb. I'm a coward. I can't even shovel in the garden right. I went out and picked a dog and the stupid thing is *blind*."

"We'll get another dog."

"No! I want *this* one!"

He sighed again. "You know, Squirt, if you try to train Skipper . . . and it doesn't work out . . . he's going to be miserable. You're going to be miserable, too. All of us will be. And then he'll be older and you'll be more attached to him and maybe God just didn't *intend* Skipper to grow up that way. Did you ever think of that? Maybe this is just one of life's disappointments. And you have to get through it and go on, and grow up to be a man."

"Oh, Dad," I said, "please don't make me give him away. Please don't take him away. Please don't have somebody put him to sleep. He'll be a good dog. I'll get him trained. He won't be miserable. I'll take care of him. I'll do everything. Honest I will! Just give me a chance! Please!"

He did not reply. He sat there with his hand on the back of my neck, his fingers stroking my hair. I smelled his tobacco and sweat, and the linty odor of his clothing. He had always, it seemed, been so busy. There had been very few times like this. I wanted to say more—how much I loved him. Loving him and feeling a fool and wanting Skipper and dreading his decision were all mixed up together, and I knew that any moment he would reach down and take Skipper out of my arms and take him away.

He did not. He sat quiet for a very long time. Skipper squirmed a little in my lap, and then slept.

Finally my father stood and looked down at us. He looked tired and enormously sad. "If you try with him, Squirt, and fail, it's going to be so much harder for all of us later."

I looked up at him, unable to speak.

"Are you really ready to risk that much more pain?" he asked.

"He'll be great, Dad. You'll see. I'll teach him *everything*."

He sighed again, seemed ready to say more. Then he turned and left the room, closing the door softly behind him.

I took Skipper to his box and put him down inside. He walked around a little, splashing in his water pan. I heard him slurping a drink. *He's learned that already. He'll be fine.*

Pulling back the sheet on the bed, I stretched out. A faint, warm breeze stirred the curtains, cooling my body. In the sky beyond the window were a million tiny stars. I wondered if there were planes up there somewhere, too, fighter pilots looking for German bombers. Tomorrow at school, I thought, Bill Sheehan would tell everyone that I had a blind dog.

None of that seemed to matter very much. Skipper was in the box beside me. I was going to have a chance.

Somewhere else in the house my mother and father were talking quietly again. I could tell by the tone that my mother was asking questions, my father calmly trying to reassure her. *He was on my side.* This realization came to me so clearly, and with such force, that I cried again. I had never done anything to deserve him. I loved him so much I could hardly stand it. If I failed him now, after he had given me this chance, I would never be able to make up for it. It seemed to me then that I had taken on a huge—a perhaps insupportable—burden.

I thought, too, about my German. *Rudi Gerhardt.* I tried his name on my tongue and thought back over every moment with him. He had not seemed all that vicious. His companion had looked like a scared kid.

This was all very complicated for me. I knew I had to hate them. But Rudi had not been lying when he spoke of training— of a dog of his own. He would be back, I thought, presenting me a choice of whether to hide and hate him or try to find other chances to speak with him so I might perhaps learn more about how to handle my Skipper. I already knew that my choice would be the pragmatic one. I felt like I might have just taken the first mental step toward becoming a traitor to my country.

In his box, Skipper whined. I reached down and petted him. He became quiet. I lay still and looked out at the stars, thinking.

7

Colonel Thatcher was, if anything, methodical, and his duty rosters ordered that identical work crews would work the same farm areas over and over. My father had said that the outside well was always available for prisoners, under proper watch, to use. For these reasons, the next days gave me more opportunities to see and briefly talk with the man I had begun to consider "my German."

"You are teaching Skipper to know your voice?" he asked.

"He must know it," I replied. "His tail always wags when I talk to him."

"Good. He must learn commands." Rudi frowned, thinking about it. "Come. This is number one. Always: 'Come.' No other word. He must obey."

"I talked to him this morning and he came right at my voice. But there was a chair in the way, and he bonked himself a good one."

Rudi smiled faintly. "Then that is what *you* must learn. You must never say to come unless the way is clear between the dog and where you stand."

"That might not be so easy," I said.

"It was never said to be easy."

"I'll *try*."

"Good. Now. Stay. This is another command. You say to stay, he must sit down and remain exactly where he is."

"That's going to be even harder!"

"Of course."

"He wants to run around all the time."

"Of course."

I looked at Rudi. "I don't know if I can *do* this."

"You can," Rudi told me. "If you want it badly enough, you can."

"I dunno."

"Then the dog must be put to sleep."

"*No!*"

"There is no middle ground. Discipline. It is the only way a dog such as this one can live. He has no eyes. His life— blackness. You are his vision. He must be taught to obey your voice and trust it as though it were his own eyes."

"I don't know how to make him obey," I admitted. "I tell him something and he does something else."

"Repetition."

"I've told him a hundred times!"

"Tell him a thousand times. Tell him one million times. Always the same. He will learn. There is no other way."

"What if he won't?" I asked despairingly. "I had him on the front porch. I had the leash on him. I pulled on it. I said to come. He knew where I was. He wanted to play. He started off the other direction and fell clear off the porch like a dodo bird!"

"When he disobeys," Rudi told me, "you must punish him."

"How?"

"Speak sternly. He will learn the tone. If he is very bad, shake him by the neck. That is how a mother teaches her pups."

"I get mad," I said.

"Of course. But you can never give in to the anger. Anger is for fools. To teach, you must be the same. Always. When he is good, reward. When he disobeys, punish."

"It doesn't seem fair," I mused. "He's already got so much trouble. And then I make him do exactly what I want."

Rudi's eyes widened slightly in surprise. "But this is universal," he told me. "It is for people, too. The more trouble—the more discipline. There is no other way."

I tried. God, how I tried. I would take the puppy into the side yard and put him on the leash. He had begun to learn that he was safe within its confines but liked to stay at the end of it, as if the tug at his neck gave him a sense of having a center. I would pull on the leash. "Skipper. Come."

More often than not he ignored me completely.

"Skipper! Come!"

Wagging his tail, he nuzzled the grass.

I pulled the string harder, stretching his neck, pulling him. "Come. *Come.*" He fought, writhing, almost getting an ear through the collar. I grabbed him and shook him roughly, making him cry.

I had to be hardhearted. "Now we'll try it again," I said in my stern voice.

He walked to the end of the leash.

"*Come.*"

Perhaps by accident, he gamboled my way. I grabbed him and hugged him and, from my pants pocket, took a piece of a cookie. He slobbered all over me with pleasure.

"You're going to learn," I told him, "if it kills both of us."

There were some heavy spring rains, and the small drainage ditch below the rise where our house sat, which I considered a creek, ran high and fast, scattering debris along its banks. Later, when the sun was out again, prisoners came in a truck to work on the channel with hand tools. When I got home from school I found them down there, and Rudi was with them. Soon a shrill whistle gave the men a break, and I pulled Skipper along on his string leash to where Rudi had slumped to a wet, fallen log.

"The dog grows," Rudi said, smiling. He looked thin and tired.

"He eats like a horse."

"Good. The training?"

"I must be making progress. I've told him to come two million times already."

"Good!" Rudi chuckled.

"He sure is hard to walk on the leash, though," I said.

"Then you must also begin teaching him to heel."

"What's that?"

"Walk at your side at all times on command."

"Oh, he'll never learn that!"

Rudi stood stiffly. "May I?" he asked, reaching for the leash.

I gave it to him and he made little kissing sounds with his mouth, tugging Skipper to his feet. He wrapped the leash around his fist several times, making it so short that Skipper could stand comfortably only when the leash was extended directly downward. If Skipper tried to move in any direction from Rudi's side, he immediately pulled himself off the ground.

Rudi stood there, letting Skipper fuss and struggle and start to learn. "Heel," he said. "Heel. Heel."

"He's learning it already!" I cried.

Rudi started walking slowly, murmuring softly in German. Skipper tried first to run ahead, and swung himself into the air, and then hung back, sitting down and getting dragged along in the wet earth. Rudi kept repeating the command softly. Skipper gave up and moved alongside him to relieve himself of the tug of the leash.

"He's already doing better!" I exclaimed. "How did you *do* that?"

"I gave him very little space in which to make a mistake. Walk him so. If he will not walk, drag him gently. He will learn to walk so that his coat lightly brushes your leg—so. Later you will give him the command and even without the leash he will walk the same."

"You must know everything there is to know about dogs!"

Rudi smiled. "A little only. Tell me. Do you have a whistle?"

"A whistle?"

"I will get one for you. I can make it."

"Rudi, did you really have a blind dog in Germany?"

"Of course."

"Do you miss her?"

"Yes."

"Where did you get captured?"

"In Africa. Near a town whose name I never knew."

"Was Africa nice?"

"Nice?" He seemed surprised. "No."

I was surprised. Africa had always sounded terribly romantic to me, and Tarzan never had any trouble finding good things to eat there. "Were you glad to get captured, then?" I asked. "So you could come to America?"

"Glad? To be captured?" For an instant his eyes hardened. "No."

"Do you like it in America?" I persisted.

He looked at me thoughtfully. "It is not a question of relevance," he said finally.

"Look," I said impatiently. "How do I know I can trust you?"

"Trust?" He studied my expression.

"I think you know what the word means."

"Of course I know what it means, Danny. But I do not understand the question."

"You're *German.* I'm American. We're supposed to be enemies. But you're helping me with Skipper. You haven't even tried to kill me one time yet."

"*Mein Gott!* Why should I want to injure *you?*"

"Because we're enemies!"

"A soldier goes to fight because it is his duty and he must obey. A soldier does not kill women and children—civilians not fighting."

"Yeah! Tell me more about your bombers, then!"

Rudi looked inexpressibly sad. "Yes. But now this is different. You can trust me, Danny. I want nothing from you."

"I still feel like it's risky," I admitted.

"Of course it is. To trust someone is always a risk."

"Then why should I do it?"

"Because you are a good boy and you cannot help yourself."

"No, because I want help with Skipper and I don't have any principles, I'll take help from *anybody*."

He smiled. "You are really a bad person, then?"

I thought of my cowardice. "You don't know, boy. You just don't know."

"Maybe one day you will tell me what you mean."

I looked at him in horror. "Never!"

The guards sounded whistles. The nearest one said, "Okay. Back to work. *Schnell*."

Rudi started to turn away.

"What was it like in Africa?" I called after him.

He looked back. "Hot. Sand. Very dry."

"What was it like in Germany?"

"Green. Cool. On the hills, forests. Along the valley across the green fields from my home, on the hillside, there was a castle, white. I walked my dogs there. Children came. We sang."

"Come on, come on," the nearest guard snapped.

Rudi turned and limped down the hill. I watched him thoughtfully. It seemed very strange to hear of green fields and a castle, and the singing of children, from this gentle man. It was very hard to square it with Stukas and the blitzkrieg and storm troopers and Hitler. I wondered if all the prisoners were like Rudi. Maybe only the nice Germans got captured.

The work on the creek took several days, and in that time I managed several more brief meetings with Rudi. Sometimes the guards were suspicious of him and stayed close, watching us as if we were co-conspirators. Most of the time they were vigilant but relaxed, and we had several minutes to talk. On one of those visits he brought me a whistle he had carved out of wood. When I blew it, I heard no sound but Skipper's ears perked up. That was how I learned about sounds dogs hear better than humans.

Rudi told me also that dogs without sight developed exceptional sense of smell, and the ability to detect movement by vibration. He also drew for me with a stick in the dirt a diagram

of a slipping clasp I could make to leave Skipper tied to a stake
so he would not tangle himself up.

"He needs more exercise than you can give," Rudi told me,
squatting with me near the garden while other prisoners downslope smoked among themselves. A guard stood not far away,
but my friendship with Rudi had become generally known now,
and there was little suspicion. "You see how large are his paws.
He is going to be big." Rudi smiled. "A fine, big dog."

"He's grown a lot already," I pointed out.

"Yes. In six weeks' time he will be large enough to go wherever he wants, even if you hold on to his rope. By then he must
be trained to do what you tell him. Or he will drag you away."

I looked at Skipper, still roly-poly with fat, but beginning to
get longer legs. "He always comes now. He's smart. He's going
to be fine."

"I hope so. Yes. There is one other thing . . ." Rudi looked
into the distance, seemed to reconsider, and stopped.

"Another thing?" I prodded.

He frowned. "Sometimes a dog with a . . . hindrance . . .
what do you say—this blindness or some other—"

"Disability."

"Disability. Yes." Rudi grinned. "You are very smart for
your age."

"I read a lot. You were saying?"

"Sometimes a dog like this is suspicious. Sometimes I have
seen a dog with bad seeing or hearing—once a dog with a missing rear leg—get mean."

"Skipper would never get mean! He likes everybody!"

"This kind of dog is very loyal to a person . . . a small
group of persons. That is normal. Good. But you should watch
him for signs of being more than that. Even vicious. If this
starts to happen, you must be sure to punish him severely. If
this thing starts, and you ignore it, the results in a grown dog
could be . . . very, very bad."

"Skipper won't ever get mean! I guarantee it!"

"I hope not."

We squatted in silence and watched Skipper nervously move
up and down the length of his rope tied to the fence post.

Something else had been on my mind, and I considered whether to ask it. Curiosity won out. "Is it okay in the camp, Rudi? I mean, do they treat you all right?"

"Fine," he said soberly. "The food is good. Good place to sleep. You do your work and not cause trouble, it is fine."

"Are you glad you got captured? So you don't have to fight anymore?"

His eyes hardened. *"Nein,"* he snapped, and for an instant he was angry with me.

"Did you *want* to keep fighting?" I asked, astonished.

"It is not a question of want. It is question of duty."

"You act like you want Germany to win this war!"

"Do you want America to win the war?"

"Sure! We're the good guys!"

He looked at me in surprise.

"Aren't we?" I asked.

He grimaced, struggling with the language. "I was . . . placed in the Army. But it is duty of every man to fight for his fatherland. When your time comes, you too will go and fight. I hope it does not happen for you. But if it does, you will go."

"Sure! I love my country!"

"I love my Germany. The same."

"Hitler? People like that?"

He sighed. "Sometimes your country has leaders you do not like. But it is still your country. There is trouble . . . war . . . you go. Fight."

"But you got captured," I said, thinking somehow that this put him on our side.

"My unit was in desert. For three days we fought. Cut off, then. No food. Then no water. Finally, no more bullets. Our tanks, burning. Our commanders, all dead. Some of us fought with knives." He gave me a hot, angry look. "When I am captured, it is because I am injured, there is no more way to fight."

"You should have given up earlier!"

"We were told to fight. A man obeys orders. He does what is to be done. For his country."

"But Hitler—"

"Even when your country is wrong, you still love your country!"

It was too much for me. I could not understand his point of view. "When the war is over," I said, "will you go back?"

"Of course," he said quickly. Then his eyes dimmed. "If there is a Germany remaining for me to go back."

"There will be, Rudi. You'll get to go back."

He smiled. "Yes. We will think that, eh?"

The whistles blew. He got up stiffly and limped back to his comrades. I saw one of them give him a sullen look and an angry burst of German. Rudi shrugged and walked by the man. Several of them glanced toward me, their eyes still angry.

It troubled me. He was a good man, a friend. But he was a *German*. In some ways we were still enemies. He was perhaps detached from his own fellow prisoners. I saw that the prisoners who were angry with him had no real problem with their situation. Neither did people like Mr. Sheehan in town. They all saw things in simple black and white.

"If you ask me," Jimmy Cantwell said one day at recess, "what they ought to do is go out to that camp with a bunch of hand grenades and just blow the whole thing up."

"Right," Bill Sheehan growled. "Or use 'em for bayonet practice."

"Wouldn't that be neat?" Phil Inright said. "Hang 'em up still kicking, and then you go at 'em with your bayonet." He demonstrated in the air, making stabbing, slashing motions. "Wow! Rip! Make their guts fall out!"

We were squatted in the gravel near the school building waiting for the signal to return to class. Of the half dozen in the group, everyone else leered at the wonderful prospect Inright proposed.

"My dad," Cantwell said, "says there's going to be trouble. He's ready. You oughtta see the guns we got. I've got my BB gun ready, too. If they ever get out of that place, we'll get our chance, boy."

Sheehan turned to me with his instinctive feel for the jugular.

"Your old man works out there. Has he killed any of them yet?"

"There hasn't been any trouble," I said. "They do good work on the farms, my dad says."

"Probably poisoning everything," Inright said.

"Yeah!" Cantwell agreed. "You won't catch *me* eating any of that stuff they work on!"

"My old man—" someone else began.

"How come your dad works out there anyway?" Inright cut in.

"It's his job."

"Is he in the Army? He ain't in the Army."

"No, it's just his job."

"I bet he gets to beat up on a lot of those Krauts," Sheehan said with relish. He pounded a fist into his palm. "Wham! I'd like to get my hands on a few of them. Boy, would *I* make them bleed!"

Everyone else nodded approvingly. I knew I should keep my big mouth shut, but as usual I did not. "They're not all that bad," I said.

"What?" Sheehan said, incredulous.

"I said, not all of them are that bad."

"Germans?"

"Germans."

Sheehan put his fists on his hips. "What are you, bud? Some kind of Nazi, on top of everything else?"

I began to sweat. "All I said was, they're not all bad guys."

"They're Germans. I hate all of 'em. If I had *my* way, we'd line 'em up and get out our machine guns and"—he imitated, jerking his knotted hands in front of him—*"ack-ack-ack-ack-ack!"*

"Yeah!" Inright grinned. *"Then* hang 'em up and let their guts fall out!"

"You're wrong," I said, goaded by my newfound knowledge. "A lot of them are just ordinary guys. You can't just hate *everybody.*"

"Is that what your old man tells you?" Sheehan asked suspiciously.

"No, that's what I know."

"Is your old man sweet on Nazis too?"

"Of course not! All I'm saying is—"

"How did your old man get that job, anyhow? Write to Hitler?"

My face flamed. "Stop talking about him like that!"

"Was he a policeman or something before?"

"No."

"How come he ain't in the Army? Too old?"

Sheehan said, "He's not too old."

"Why ain't he in the Army, then?" Inright asked, eyes narrowed with suspicion.

"He's 4-F," I said. "He's got something wrong with him. It's nothing serious, but it's—"

"Probably flat feet." Cantwell grinned. "And a coward."

"Yeah," Sheehan said. "Like father like son, huh, Flatfoot?"

"You take it back," I said.

"You want to make something of it?"

I looked at him, torn between anger and cowardice. "You just take it back," I said weakly.

He scrambled to his feet, dancing around, head ducked behind his shoulder, thumbing at his nose. "Come on! Come on! Make me take it back!"

I cringed, unmoving.

"Come on," Sheehan panted, dancing and weaving. "Come on! You're yellow. You're a yellow flatfoot. Come on!"

I looked up at him. He looked so stupid, so brimming with childish bravado, that I might have laughed if I had not been terrified. It made things infinitely worse for me to see so clearly that he was a fool, yet be so frightened. "I don't want to fight," I said thickly.

Behind us, the school bell clangored loudly.

Sheehan moved close and bounced a fist off the top of my head. The bright pain rocked me back. "You'll fight," he said. "Sooner or later, Flatfoot, you'll fight."

I got up slowly as the others headed for the doors. My vision was blurry with angry tears, which made my humiliation more complete. In the classroom, everything seemed normal. I went through the remainder of the afternoon sure that they would get me afterward. Benny Harrison was my only hope. I scrambled fast to get into departure line beside him. We went out together, across the school yard, toward the street crossing where he would go his way and I would board the bus. I saw the smaller kids already boarding. We marched behind the school guards with their white chest belts and flags on bamboo poles.

"You're going to have to fight him," Benny told me without preamble.

"Fight who?" I asked as if surprised.

"Don't give me that crap. You know who."

"I don't want to fight him."

"You scared?"

"What if I am?"

"He's not so tough. You can probably lick him."

"What if I don't?"

"Well, then he probably kills you," Benny said philosophically.

"I don't know anything about fighting."

"Didn't your pop ever teach you?"

"No."

"Didn't you have to fight in Columbus?"

"That was different. I started in that school. I was always just one of the guys."

"So you didn't have to fight," Benny said. "Well, it's different here. The new kid fights. That's it. That's the way they run it."

"If I hadn't tried to be a big shot, and wear boots like yours—"

"Yeah, that was stupid. But they would have tried you out anyway."

"But I don't *want* to fight!"

"Well, that don't matter. You got to. Then they'll either leave you alone or you'll be dead. That's the way things are."

We crossed the street. The buses were waiting. I looked at Benny. "Are there books about fighting?"

"Kid, you don't learn fighting in no *book*."

"Then I don't know what I'm going to do."

"I'll tell you what. Why don't you come to my house some day after school? I'll give you a lesson and we can smoke some cigarettes."

"Would you do *that?* Gosh!"

"Sure," Benny said, his hard eyes flicking over the crowd. "You could come stay the night. My old lady won't mind."

"I'll do it," I said. "Thanks, Benny! Thanks a lot!"

He shrugged, making some of the trinkets on his cap jingle, turned, and walked away.

I climbed on the bus. Aggie was already there, surrounded by friends. I got a seat next to a girl by the window and pretended to fall asleep. Inright and Cantwell got on, made a Flatfoot remark, and went to the back. Inright stole a girl's book and tossed it to Cantwell, creating a commotion. I stayed out of it. I felt secret elation. I imagined myself standing over a fallen Bill Sheehan, being magnanimous in victory. Sheehan's nose was bleeding and everyone was in awe. My imagination was slightly defective. In my mind-picture, I kept looking like Benny Harrison.

When we got home that day, Mother had some fresh cookies. Aggie and I sat at the kitchen table dunking them in milk. Her kittens, rapidly becoming cats, played on the floor. Outside, Skipper paced on his rope.

"Mom," I said, "do you suppose I could stay a night at a friend's house?"

"I imagine you could, dear," she said. "One of your new friends from school?"

"Yessum."

"Is it all right with his mother?"

"Well, he's going to check."

"All right. We'll ask your father tonight. What's the boy's name?"

"Benny," I said.

"Benny what?"

"Harrison."

"All right, dear. We'll ask your father tonight."

Aggie, meanwhile, had done a double-take at Benny's name.

When we finished the cookies and I headed outside, she tagged after me. *"You're* going to Benny Harrison's house?" she demanded accusingly.

"What's it to you?"

"Do you know Benny Harrison is the meanest boy in school?"

"He's tough. He isn't mean."

"Same thing."

"No, it's not."

"I'm going to tell."

"Aggie, don't. Please."

"Why shouldn't I?" she asked with her smuggest expression.

"Because I'm asking you. Aggie, Benny isn't a bad guy. All I want to do is go visit him."

"Why? He's mean and he smokes and people say he steals things and he plays hooky and he's *awful*. Why do you want to visit him?"

"If I tell you, will you keep quiet?"

She glared at me.

"He's going to teach me how to fight," I said.

Her eyes widened. "So you can beat up Bill Sheehan?"

"Maybe," I hedged.

"Goody!" She grinned, clapping her hands. "I won't tell anybody *anything!"*

I breathed relief. "I'll work with Skipper now."

She tagged along. Skipper heard us coming. He went to his belly and growled. It was the first time he had ever done this and he looked menacing despite his youth. Remembering Rudi's statements, I chilled.

"Oh, you stop that, you dummy," Aggie said blithely, walking right up to him. "Can't you hear or smell who we are?" And Skipper rolled over on his back, wagging all over. My relief was intense.

When he got home that evening, my father was excited and upset. It seemed that two of the prisoners had walked away from their work detail near Grove City. They had not been missed until the truck got back to the camp and rosters were being checked routinely.

"We're trying to keep it quiet," he told us, "but we've notified Fort Hayes and the governor's office. The state police are looking, too."

"But you've always said there's no danger," my mother said, pale.

"I don't think there is any danger. But I didn't think they would walk away, either."

"Where do they think they can *go?*"

"God knows," my father said grimly.

As it turned out later that night, the escape had been a comedy of errors. The two prisoners had been in a washroom at the side of the road in a tourist rest stop when the trucks pulled out for the next job. Leaving the washroom and finding themselves abandoned, the prisoners—a forty-six-year-old man and a twenty-year-old boy—had been in a panic. They tried hitchhiking, and an unsuspecting farmer had taken them in his truck into the village of Grove City. There they had gone to the police station to surrender, but all the police had been working a funeral. Sitting on the police station porch for three hours, because the funeral ran into the supper hour for the chief, they had been "captured" by a drugstore owner waving a Colt .45 and two area farmers with shotguns. They were shaking all over by the time soldiers got them back to the safety of the camp.

We heard the story from the colonel, who was not amused.

"Well"—my father smiled with relief when the colonel had finished telling us late that night in our living room—"all's well that ends well."

"Possibly," the colonel snapped. He was wearing fatigues and a bone-handled revolver strapped around his middle, a steel helmet with his eagle on the front. "Nevertheless, this demonstrates laxity in our security. I want things tightened up, Davidson."

"We'll have a meeting of the drivers and the guards," my father said.

"I intend to issue new directives," the colonel said, pacing. "Guards are to shoot to kill."

My father looked shocked. "You just said yourself that this was more an accident than anything else."

"Granted. But we must consider the psychological effects both on the prisoners and the populace at large. A strong statement, showing we won't hesitate to take the most severe action, will make sure no one tries a real escape. And it will reassure the citizenry of Harmony."

"A lot of people are panicky about the prisoners already," my father argued. "Such a statement could be misread—increase tension."

"I think that's for me to decide, Davidson," the colonel snapped.

Anger flickered in my father's eyes and was quickly extinguished. "Yes, sir."

The colonel gave him a hard stare. "You don't agree."

"I'm afraid, sir, that such an order might cause resentment among the prisoners. They've behaved very, very well. Also, instead of reassuring the populace, such a statement might fan fears—make it sound like the danger is greater than it is."

The colonel glowered. "I see your line. However, I disagree with it. Stern action, Davidson; that's the ticket. Keep them in line. I've made my decision. We'll stand formation at oh-seven-hundred tomorrow and I'll announce the decision personally. A little show of force never hurt in a situation such as this."

My father and mother unhappily saw him to the door. His staff jeep drove away, its lights receding into the vast country night. My parents came back into the living room where I was piled up in a chair with the plans for a new model.

"He'll cause trouble," my father said. "*Damn!*"

"Maybe it won't be so bad," my mother said.

"I don't know. We've bent over backward to be fair. The men have recognized it . . . respected us for it. That town in there is an armed camp just aching for some sign of trouble. There are some tough ones among the prisoners. Give them mistreatment . . . unfairness . . . as an excuse—"

"Isn't there some way you could stop the colonel?" I asked.

My father looked surprised. "No—how?"

"Doesn't he have a boss at Fort Hayes? Couldn't you tell the boss the colonel is doing wrong?"

"No. Of course not. That's out of the question."

"*Why?*"

"It just *is*, Squirt. You owe loyalty to your superior."

My thoughts were of Rudi working in front of trigger-happy guards. "Don't you owe the prisoners something too, though?"

"You don't understand this."

"I'll tell you what, though. I think you ought to go tell the colonel's general, or whatever he is, in Columbus! I—"

"And lose my job?" my father said sharply, angry.

I looked at him, and it was my turn to be shocked. He was afraid for his job—*afraid of the colonel*. My dad was afraid! It took my breath away.

"I burned my bridges when we came out here," he said, half to me, half to my mother. "I have to make good at this. I can't go off half cocked and risk everything!"

"Of course you can't," my mother said. "And probably it won't be nearly as risky as he made it sound. I'm sure everything will be fine, George. Really."

He did not reply. Quietly I gathered up my plans and went to my bedroom. I was shaken. My father—my own father—was going to be a party to a bad thing. I did not know how to deal with this. I sat in my room and watched the airplanes turn on their strings and wondered what trouble lay ahead for all of us.

8

There was in the country in those days a feeling that I remember vividly because it was so beautiful and because we may never experience it as a nation again. My childish feeling that I should hate all enemies of the country was not at the heart of what was going on in our patriotism. At the center was a sense of all of us pulling together, absolutely united in our love of America. Whether we were worrying about the date of the next ration stamp, buying war bonds, studying the news in the evening newspaper, or balling our tinfoil, we knew that everyone else was pulling with us, and that our cause was just. We saw films of another Kaiser Liberty Ship sliding down the ways, and Rosie the Riveter waving to the camera, and we felt *we* had had a part in that, too. We sent trucks through town to collect scrap aluminum, and took it quite seriously when told that Lucky Strike green had gone to war. Our vocabularies filled with new sounds: panzers and bazookas, Colin Kelly and George Patton, Bataan, Corregidor, El Alamein, and Anzio. Strangers winked on the street and gave the V for Victory sign. And sometimes at night, as darkness spread over the great land,

we turned on radios and listened to President Roosevelt, and
believed in him.

We knew our cause was just. America was *us:* us in Washington and New York City and Miami and Harlem and Denver
and Chicago, and in Norman, Oklahoma, and Harmony, Ohio,
too. *We* the people. What a sound it had then! It has taken
many terrible things to tear that faith out of our hearts. Now
those who did not live those years can scarcely imagine how
unified and proud of our heritage we really were. I mourn the
change. For those days, and that feeling of unity and purpose,
were priceless.

Colonel Thatcher made his hard-line speech to the massed
prisoners that next day. But almost at once his action began to
backfire on him, and to have the negative results my father
evidently feared. Later that same day, a prisoner was late getting back to a work detail after drawing water. A soldier
pushed him, knocking him down. The prisoner attacked. The
guard knocked him out with the butt of his rifle. The same day,
two other prisoners got in a fight between themselves in the
compound. Civilian guards intervened with bayonets on their
rifles and one of the prisoners ended up in the hospital with
a serious wound in his abdomen. The colonel decreed ten days
in the stockade, in solitary confinement, for both the prisoner
who had attacked the guard and the healthy one who had been
fighting.

Word of the "escape" to Grove City, meanwhile, was
through Harmony like a wildfire. By the time it was repeated at
my school grounds, the escapees, so-called, had taken the
farmer's truck after beating him severely, and had been caught
trying to break into the jail to steal weapons and ammunition.
There was a story, Jimmy Cantwell said, that German submarines were everywhere off the East Coast, and secret radio messages had been sent to all prisoners to break out and get to
New Jersey, where rubber boats would pick them up.

Over the next few days, other stories spread. I was told that
the prisoners were in radio communications with the Third
Reich, and Hitler himself had called upon them to break out

and destroy America from within. This story, repeated solemnly by Phil Inright, had it that prisoners everywhere were to seize their captors' weapons and fight their way into control of local towns and cities, creating island fortresses all over the United States. This would create such chaos in America that the Army and Marines would have to fight on our own land for weeks or even months, completely disrupting the war effort overseas. By the next Sunday, the first of June, the Columbus *Dispatch* felt called upon to run a major feature story with many pictures purporting to show how secure the camp really was.

"They're lying," Bill Sheehan said Monday. "They just don't want folks to know how dangerous things are. Where there's smoke, there's fire!"

I knew he was wrong—maybe—but I did not contradict him. I knew it would only end with him thumbing his nose and dancing around me again as I cowered.

That same week was the week of the big practice blackout in central Ohio. It coincided with my long-awaited visit to Benny Harrison's house.

The practice air-raid blackout, scheduled for a Thursday night, had been well publicized, and was being taken very seriously. Everyone knew that Columbus and its environs would be a prime target for the *Luftwaffe* if and when the Stukas and Junkers decided to strike. Columbus, after all, had the Bolt Works, Timken Roller Bearings, Fort Hayes, and the Depot, a huge army storage facility where all the saddles and gas masks from World War I were still in storage. To outsiders, Columbus might not look like a major target, the wisdom went, but local people *knew*. The *Luftwaffe* was no bunch of dummies. And Harmony, being on the outskirts, was just as vulnerable.

Elaborate plans had been made for the practice and they were posted everywhere in town that afternoon when I walked home with Benny for my visit and boxing lesson. I was glad I would be in town where the action was. Benny, as usual, was not impressed.

"The way I figure it," he said, "if they come over here, everybody will just get out their rifles and shotguns and shoot them down. They probably don't know how many people around here are loaded for bear."

"Those bombers are pretty fast, Benny."

"Yeah? Well, so's my Uncle Jess with his ten-gauge, boy!"

We had left the school and walked east, through the small business district, then along a block sloping downhill, with pool halls and automotive repair shops, to the river. Here the Big Walnut wended its way through town, grassy banks punctuated by parallel railroad tracks, some metal industrial buildings, and grain elevators. The steel bridge over the river carried both cars and pedestrians, and we could feel the structure vibrate from traffic as we crossed it. The Big Walnut was almost a hundred yards wide below.

"It's a big old river here," I observed.

"Creek, really," Benny corrected. "But you'll think it's a river the first time it floods."

"It floods?" I said, thrilled.

"Every once in a while. It hasn't for years, but I've heard it once covered the whole business district over there." He grinned fiendishly. "If it does it again, bang! There goes the school!"

We walked on to his house, one of a few dozen in a row on a dirt street behind a sprawling junk yard. An old Ford rusted into the weeds in his side yard. On a rickety swing on the front porch sat a heavy, smiling blond woman wearing shorts and a halter.

"This your friend?" she asked, putting down a bottle of beer.

"Yeah," Benny said. "Danny Davidson. Danny, this is my old lady."

His mother winced as she untangled long, pale legs and got to her feet. She tugged at her short shorts, making herself more presentable. "Hi, Danny. Tell him he ought to have more respect for his mother. 'Old lady' indeed!"

"Pleased to meet you, I'm sure," I said, shaking hands.

"There," she told Benny. "You see that? Manners. Real nice manners. Why can't you be more like that?"

"Aah, baloney," Benny growled.

"It's kind of warm, boys. Do you want something to drink?"

"Yeah!" Benny grinned. "How about a coupla beers?"

She gave him an affectionate swat, took us into the house, and poured us green Kool-Aid. I looked around the kitchen in fascination as we drank. Every inch of sinkboard was covered with dirty dishes. The trash can brimmed with empty beer bottles. Where a heating pipe should have gone through the ceiling, there was some newspaper taped over the hole. I could smell leaking natural gas.

"You go to school with Benny, Danny?" his mother asked, sitting with us.

"Yessum," I said. "We're in the same room."

"That's nice," she told me. "It's nice for a boy to have a friend. Are you a class officer too?"

I glanced at Benny, not wanting to mess up whatever lie he had told her. "No, ma'am. I'm new."

"Well," she beamed, "you stick with my Benny, and if he ever gets tired of being president, maybe he'll fix you up in some high office. Right, Benny?"

"Aah," Benny growled.

She sighed. "It's almost time for me to go to work. No rest for the wicked." She gave me what I could only interpret as a strangely flirtatious glance. "Right?"

"Right," I agreed.

She got up and left the room, pale legs twinkling.

"What a dodo," Benny muttered.

"That's no way to talk about your mom!" I told him.

"You can feed her anything and she'll believe it," he said disgustedly.

"Did you tell her you're class president?"

"Sure. Why not?"

"What if she goes to school and finds out it's not so?"

"Her? Go to school? Are you kidding? She'd have to put out some effort to do that."

"Benny," I said, more shocked, "you ought to talk nicer about your own mother."

"Aah," he grunted, "so what? You know where she works? She works downtown in a beer joint. She says she waits tables, only onct I went down there and looked in. She wears this frilly costume bare up to her butt, and her top practically hanging out."

"Benny!"

"Well, it's true. So what difference? My old man left her. He got smart. One of these days I'll take off, too. So what?"

"You shouldn't talk that way! She's . . . real nice. She loves you!"

"Kid, you got a lot to learn. In this world *nobody* loves you. It's dog eat dog and the devil take the hindmost."

"I could never believe that, Benny. It's—"

"Yeah! And that's why you spend so much time on your butt in the playground, too! Now come on. Drink up. We'll go out back and see if we can't teach you a few things about beating people up."

We went into the back yard, which was a patch of barren earth bounded by a rusty metal fence, an enormous grape arbor, and a garage with most of the paint peeled off. The faint smell of mildew pervaded. Benny removed his beanie and squared off with me in the middle of the dirt.

"The first mistake most people make fighting," he told me, "is trying to be nice. In a fight you don't be nice. If you can stay out of a fight, good. But if you can't, what you want is the shortest fight possible. Now. You got three basic kinds of fights. Guys a lot smaller than you, guys a lot bigger than you, and guys your own size, almost. With the little guy, no problem. You move in fast and aim for the nose. Bust his nose and he'll bleed like crazy and run off. With a guy a lot bigger, what you want to do is look for a board or a brick and hit him right between the eyes with it, and then run."

"What if he catches you?" I asked.

Benny shrugged. "Then you get beat up. That happens sometimes. But let's talk about guys near your own size, like Sheehan or Inright."

"Inright is a foot taller!" I protested.

"He's blubber, too. Okay. Now. The trick is, the other guy almost always dances around, getting ready. You don't wait.

You attack. Got it? Okay." He assumed a fighting stance. "I'm Sheehan, wanting you to fight. What are you going to do?"

"Attack?" I said weakly.

"Then *do* it! Come on!"

I wanted very much to please him, and learn. I rushed him. He made a sharp little movement and something bright and painful exploded on the point of my chin. I saw yellow stars and sat down in the dirt.

Benny looked down at me thoughtfully. "I forgot to mention you don't just run in with your hands at your sides. You cover up and you hit with your fists. Okay. Try again."

I got up slowly. He danced around me. It occurred to me that this had to be one of the world's great insane spectacles, *me* attacking Benny Harrison. I hesitated. Benny moved. Before I knew what was happening, he bounced against me. Yellow stars exploded in my brain again. I found myself sitting in the dirt with blood in my mouth.

Benny helped me up. His expression was sad. "I said attack *first*. You stood around with your teeth in your mouth. Even a dopus like Bill Sheehan will get you if you stand around. Try again."

I rushed, a wild anger in me. He caught my blows against his hands, dancing around me. I whirled both arms like a dervish, and a blow never landed.

"Good!" he coached, blocking my roundhouse right. "Hey! Nice one!" as my left uppercut *almost* didn't get blocked on his elbow. "Come on, now! Don't look around for cheers, man! You gotta keep coming! But you got to remember to *keep your guard up*–!" Wham! More stars. Down I went again.

He reached down a hand to help me up. "I'm sorry, kid. Some things you got to–"

I lashed out with my foot. It caught him low in the abdomen. The wind gushed out of him and he staggered backward, doing his own pratfall in the dirt. His face was contorted with pain.

I stared, horrified. Now he would kill me. "Benny! I'm sorry! I–"

His grimace changed to a grin that went ear to ear. "Great!" he told me. "Boy, that really hurt! I never even gave you a lesson yet in kicking the guy in the buns, and it came natural to you! Hey, there might be hope for you yet!"

He scrambled up, brushing himself off. "Now come on. Let's go again."

I got up and faced him.

"Of course you did make one bad mistake there," he told me, blocking a wild right.

"Huh?" I panted, trying again to get through to him.

"You had me," he said, easily parrying another left and popping me lightly on the nose. "I was down. For a few seconds I was defenseless. That was when you should have jumped right into me with both feet and finished me off."

"You?" I said. "I could never do *that*. And you don't hit a guy when he's down. It's—"

He blasted me on the side of the head, knocking me into the grape arbor. I staggered out and he hit me again, then stopped and wagged a stern finger at me. "Don't talk stupid," he said. "The purpose in a fight is to *get it over*. You get a guy down, you cream him, right?"

"Right," I muttered, and bounced another right off his elbow.

We went at it a while longer. When we were both breathing hard and sweaty, he put me down again, almost gently, and suggested a break. We went into the garage. There was a very old car rusting into the dirt floor, some belts and hoses hanging down from rafters, a greasy workbench covered with rusty tools. Benny went over to the workbench and moved some things around and produced a pack of Pall Malls. He removed one and tossed it to me, lit his, slid down to a sitting position on the floor, and waited. I tried to tap the cigarette the way my father always did. It didn't seem to accomplish anything.

"Here," Benny said, and tossed me the matches.

I lit the cigarette. It had a weedy, bitter taste. I didn't like it much. Benny drew deep on his, taking the smoke into his lungs. I tried it and coughed, fire all the way down my throat.

"They're pretty strong," Benny told me, smiling.

"Yeah!" I rasped.

"Wings are better, but you can't hardly get Wings."

"Who sells you cigarettes?" I asked.

"Nobody."

"Then?"

"I hook 'em."

I stared at him. "You go in a store and hook cigarettes?"

"Well, they won't sell 'em to me. What am I supposed to do? Pick up butts off the street?"

"Good gosh, Benny! If they catch you, it's reform school for sure!"

"Yeah, I know. That's why I don't ever get caught."

"You *hook things* in the store?" I still could not believe it.

"Just cigarettes and candy," he said. "And sometimes pop. But that's hard, boy. Things have to be just perfect before you can get pop out. Hey, you want some candy? I've got Hersheys, Baby Ruths—"

"No!" I said quickly. "I mean—I'm full, still, from lunch."

He slumped back against the wall. "Okay."

We smoked in silence. He seemed to enjoy it. I began to feel a little dizzy and also perhaps a bit nauseated. I was glad when he stubbed his butt in the sandy garage floor, allowing me to do the same. The smoke taste was foul in my mouth and my lips were beginning to swell from the pounding he had given me.

"What do you say we go in and see my room before we go again?" he asked as we left the garage.

It was fine with me. We entered the house, which seemed empty. His room was in the back. The bed was unmade and there were clothes all over the floor. I smelled cat. He had a couple of flying models on strings across a corner and another on a card table in the corner in an early stage of construction.

"What do you think?" he asked, flipping a Hurricane with his finger.

"Real nice," I said carefully. In truth it was an awful-looking model. It appeared that he had followed instructions well enough up to the time of gluing the tissue paper skin on the body and wings, but then everything had gone wrong. The paper was much too loose, full of wrinkles, and then he had spread dope on it, making the wrinkles permanent. I politely didn't mention it.

"Actually," he said, staring at the model under construction, "I like building them all right up to covering 'em. I can't never get the paper stuck on right. Wrinkles on me bad. Maybe you noticed."

"Yes, I did," I said.

"I don't know how guys get it strung over the fuselage so tight and smooth," he said. "I try it and it just tears."

"Well, how much water do you spray on?"

He looked blank. "Water?"

"Benny, you mean you don't know about spraying water on the tissue paper after it's glued to make it *shrink?*"

He made a face. "Shrink?"

For the next hour I demonstrated. He watched in silent amazement as I glued paper on a wing he had finished, then sprinkled tap water onto the tissue. It sagged even worse at first, but we put it on the sunny window sill. A little later it began to dry, shrinking and tightening. By luck it was one of my best efforts, and when it quickly dried, the thin paper stretched over the balsa-wood members like the finest steel.

Benny stared in disbelief. "Water," he said. "Plain old water." He gave me a look different from all he had given before. "You're all right, do you know that? You are really smart."

"It's just a trick," I said modestly.

He put his arm around my shoulders. "Come on. Let's go back out and practice some more."

We did, and I didn't do any better. But he didn't hit me so hard this time to remind me of my mistakes.

Later we listened to the radio awhile, and it started to get dark. Out of the refrigerator he produced some bread and cold meat and we ate sandwiches on the front porch, watching traffic go by. Darkness came. At ten, the town's sirens wailed, and we made sure all the lights were off and then climbed up on the roof of the house to watch. There were a few stars between clouds overhead and we could make out the river, the darkness of city buildings beyond. We could not see a light. On the next street we could see the occasional glow of a cigarette on someone's porch, and in the vast silence could be heard people talking softly, as if the Germans would hear if they raised their voices.

It thrilled me, to tell the truth, sitting on that roof still warm from the day's sun, seeing how well Harmony complied with the blackout regulations. German bombardiers would not find Columbus tonight if everyone did as well as we were doing. I was proud to be an American.

"I hope it don't end too soon," Benny said thoughtfully.

"The blackout?"

"The war."

"Some people say ten or twenty years."

"I hope so."

"Why?"

"I want to go."

I looked at his slender silhouette in the dark. "You want to go be in it, you mean? I guess we all do. It's an honor to fight for America."

"I'm a good fighter. I could be important. People might get to know my name."

"People know your name, Benny."

"A hero," he said. "I could be a hero. Like that."

"People know your name already."

"I'm nothing," he said. "My old man run off and my old lady works in a beer joint with her things hanging out. I can't learn."

"In school, you mean? Well, Benny, if you didn't act the fool—"

"No," he said somberly. "I tried. For a long time. I did." He tapped his forehead. "There's something wrong in the upper story."

"Aw!"

"There is. I look at a page and the letters all scramble up on me. I get to where I don't even know whether to start frontward or backward, the letters are going all directions. So I said the hell with it."

"Benny, if there really is a problem, maybe a doctor or somebody could help."

"Fat chance."

"Did you ever tell anybody?"

"No. Never."

"You should!"

"No. And if you ever tell anybody, I'll kill you."

"I won't, Benny, not if you don't want me to. But if you've got an eyesight problem or something, and somebody could help—"

"Nope," he said more firmly. "It don't matter. I'm nobody anyhow. It's okay. I don't care. As long as I act like I won't learn, nobody will ever know I *can't*. So that's fine. And maybe the war will make it okay. Maybe it'll last long enough for me to get into it—be a hero. Did you ever think about being a hero?"

"Some," I admitted.

"I think about it all the time," Benny told me.

I did not reply. Here I was with one of the guys most feared and perhaps disliked in our entire school, if not the town. *I knew he did some bad things.* But he was my friend. And now here underneath the bravado and the toughness was this scared kid, crippled in some mysterious way, dreaming of heroism. He was nothing like he appeared on the surface.

In a way, I saw, he was like Rudi, my German. He had complicated my life. I almost wished I were still stupid, the way I had been when I first came to Harmony. Then I had hated all Germans and Japanese, and knew people like Benny Harrison were nothing but trash to be avoided. It had been so very simple. Now everything was so complex. I had to try to judge people one at a time, rather than in bunches. Life was never going to be easy for me again.

Benny lit another cigarette. We sat together on the roof and watched the darkness.

As June and the end of school neared, Skipper began to come around.

He was growing wonderfully. His parentage now was clear, and it had been nearly purebred shepherd. He was black, with typical shepherd tan on his shoulders, along the sides of his neck, and on his left front leg and paw. A collar of silvery white adorned his throat and chest, and touched parts of his large, bushy tail. His ears stood straight now when he was listening, head erect, every muscle taut with attention. When he ran to me and stood with his front paws on my shoulders, as he loved to do, he staggered me.

His training had come further than I might have earlier hoped. He came promptly to the sound of my voice. If I told him to stay, he stayed—at least until he thought I was out of view. He had begun to heel properly much of the time.

In addition, he had begun to learn things on his own. In the yard, when freed, he now knew how to walk entirely around the house, sniffing furiously, and often came back precisely to the stake that held his rope. If he wandered out across the grass toward the driveway, and encountered gravel beneath his paws, he turned and tried to reverse his course. In the house he had learned how to leave my room, come out through the hall, carefully pick his way around my father's chair and ottoman, and move to a favorite spot on the bare floor under a window, where he often lay for hours at a time, listening.

I was enormously proud of him, and as I counted down the days until school would be out, I imagined the expeditions into the fields and woods we would take during the hot months.

"We'll have a great time, Skipper!" I told him, nestling my face in his luxurious fur. "You're going to like it!"

If I have given the impression that school for me was complete misery, I have misled you. There were days of sheer fun, like the time in May when we worked in art class on plaster of Paris figurines to have ready for our fathers on Father's Day, casting, shaping, and then staining the small figures of a horse's head or the figure of a Collie dog. Mrs. Broadus was stern and often humorless, but at times like these she relaxed, smiling, and showed genuine affection for some of us. The class picnic at Harmony Park, near the river, was another good day. The entire school attended, each class making its own plans. I took a sheet of brownies and pan of baked beans, and Aggie took sugar cookies and Kool-Aid for her group. We ate, ran, played softball, ate again, played capture the flag and pitched horseshoes, and had a taste of adventure when a third-grader slipped on the grassy embankment of the river and fell in. A teacher named Harris went in after the boy instantly and pulled him out, frightened but healthy. The scent of near disaster made the day, and we all trooped back to school in the evening happy and thoroughly worn out.

On more routine days I was not regularly the focus of hostile attention. The name "Flatfoot" was stuck permanently on me now, and Sheehan and his best pals never looked at me except with derision or threat. The only times I became the specific focus was when my old nemesis, my own careless mouth, betrayed me.

I could not seem to keep my mouth shut at critical times.

"It's all the bombs," Cantwell said morosely one rainy day when we were all standing around the boys' room with nothing to do during recess. "Dropping all the bombs, it shakes the world on its axis, makes the weather all weird."

Everyone else nodded sagely, but I had to pipe up, "That's ridiculous, Jim. Do you have any idea how *big* the planet is? You could explode all the bombs we've got at the same time and you couldn't budge the earth on its axis!"

As a result of that brilliant reply, they took my lunch and flushed it down the toilet, and then after school Cantwell, Sheehan, and Inright tried to waylay me on the trip to the bus. I ran from them and hid in the bus in abject terror and mortification while the old man who was substitute driver that day protected me.

"Mrs. Broadus must be sixty years old," Sheehan said another time.

"Why, she can't be over thirty!" I said before thinking.

"Are you calling me a liar, Flatfoot?"

"No! No! What I meant was—"

Going back from lunch, Sheehan later walked up to me and spurted a mouthful of cold water on me. After I got excused to go dry off, somebody stole my paint box. When I fearfully insisted to Mrs. Broadus that I had lost the paints, I spent the rest of the day on the dunce chair. Every time she turned her back, Sheehan hit me with a spitball.

"They're everyplace!" Inright said another time, speaking of German submarines. "They've been sighted in the Olentangy River and Buckeye Lake!"

I *knew,* for a split second that time, that I ought to keep my trap shut. I simply could not. "That's the dumbest thing I ever heard!"

On the playground that afternoon they helped the bigger boys capture me during capture the flag. They took me down the slope behind the school and tied me to a tree. It took me two hours to get loose. By that time, school was almost over for the day. I decided the best thing to do was creep around to the bus stop and pretend I had been ill all afternoon. I got to the bus stop and saw a familiar figure churning angrily across the street to intercept me. The principal.

"What do you have to say for yourself?" he demanded angrily.

"I'm sick," I said.

"Detention," he said.

If it had not been for a poor kid named Kyler in our class, it might have been a lot worse. Looking back, I know that Kyler was retarded. At the time he seemed merely invincibly dumb. When Mrs. Broadus called on him to read, it was agony as he stood there, his bland, broad face straining, each word coming out as if dragged by meathooks. He thought Switzerland was in West Virginia. Mrs. Broadus was a fiend for the times tables. She drilled us on them endlessly. Poor Kyler never got one right.

"Kyler? Six times six!"

"Uh . . ."

"Come on, now!" She would smile encouragingly. "That's an easy one! Six times six—and six is part of the answer, Kyler!"

"Thirteen?"

As a result, some of our leaders' cruelty was vented on poor Kyler. Once they took the meat out of the sandwich in his lunch and put in the cardboard backing from a Big Chief tablet. Kyler chewed each bite a long time. On another occasion they poured ink in his thermos bottle. Once they managed to take every screw out of his desk during lunch hour so that when he came back and sat down, the desk disintegrated under him. Often during his labored recitations Mrs. Broadus would whirl to the blackboard to scrawl something likely to help him. At such times the air around his head was filled with so many spitballs it looked like the Battle of Britain. During a school play that we were entirely in charge of, Sheehan fiendishly gave Kyler a soliloquy to recite. It took poor Kyler seven minutes to get through it. Once after school, Inright and Cantwell told Kyler there was time for a quick game of hide and seek. He was sent to the toilet with instructions to count to a hundred by ones. By the time he got to a hundred, he had missed his bus.

To my eternal shame, I took part in some of these escapades.

Twice during the warming days of early June I went home again with Benny Harrison. On the second occasion he took me a different way. I found us standing across the street from a grocery.

"You want to learn something, kid?" Benny asked. "Come on and I'll show you how to hook stuff."

"*Now?*" I asked, startled.

"Sure. Come on. It's easy."

"No," I said huskily. "I—I don't feel so good, Benny. Maybe—"

"All right," he sneered. "Just stand there, then."

Before I could reply, he was walking jauntily across the street. I stood against the front of the post office and watched him enter the big A&P. It seemed a busy time, a Wednesday, many farmers' trucks in the parking lot.

Benny was inside for a long time. I sweated, knowing he had been captured. I watched for the police car to come and take him away. It was agony not only for Benny but for myself. Had I betrayed him by refusing to go with him? Would he tell the police I was his cohort, and would I too go to jail? *What would my parents say?*

After an eternity, the door of the A&P swung back and Benny walked out. He still walked as jauntily as before. In his hand he had a small sack of peanuts. He popped them into his mouth singly as he watched traffic, crossed the street, and joined me.

"Ready?" he asked, popping another peanut.

We walked around the corner and headed for the bridge. "Boy!" I exclaimed at last. "You really had me worried there! You got some peanuts, huh? But you paid for them, right? I mean, you walked right out with them." My relief was intense.

"Sure," Benny said. "You always pay for *something.*"

I looked at him, afraid of what his words meant.

With a smirk, he dug into his left pants pocket. Out came a slightly mangled Hershey bar and a package of jellybeans. Thrusting them at me, he got into his right-side pocket and took out a pack of Pall Malls. To my horror, he slit the pack, took out a cigarette, cracked a wooden match on the seat of his corduroy knickers, and started smoking.

"Eat up," he told me. "Plenty more where that came from."

Before I could reply, a vast shadow descended on us from the rear. A big, rough hand seized my arm, the other hand grabbing Benny so hard at the same time that the cigarette fell out of his mouth.

The big man, his face red and contorted with anger, was still wearing his butcher's apron. He slammed me and Benny against the wall of the building we had been passing, grabbed the cigarettes and candy in a single motion, and pinned us deeper against the bricks.

"Have you punks got a sales slip for this stuff?" he demanded.

It was almost five o'clock before my father, his face the color of ashes, strode into the little police station. Sitting on the wood bench beside the door to the cells, I felt my soul shrivel.

The police chief was grim. "Benny had been watched before," he told my father. "This time they caught him with the goods."

The store manager, he went on, was convinced that I had not taken part in the stealing, and might not even have known what Benny was up to. The store manager was going to press juvenile charges against Benny. It had been agreed in conference that perhaps I deserved the benefit of the doubt. I was being released in my parents' custody.

"There will be no . . . charges?" my father asked, his lips white and almost unmoving.

"Not this time," the chief rumbled. "But I suggest you have a good talk with this boy. He's not very smart in choosing his companions."

"You can be sure of that, sir," my father said.

The chief turned to me. "I don't know what you had in mind, Danny. But this time you were lucky. The next time, you won't be. We know you now. Get in trouble again and it's curtains. Do you understand that?"

"Yes, sir!" I choked. "I'll never even go near the A&P again!"

"Choose your playmates more careful, you hear? Boys like Harrison are no good. Do you understand that?"

"Yes, sir! I sure see *now* he's no good!"

The chief frowned at me a long time. "All right, then," he said finally.

"Are we free to go?" my father asked.

"Yes, sir. And I'm sorry this had to happen."

My father gripped my arm with a painful intensity. "Come on."

"What about Benny?" I asked.

"Boy," the chief said sternly, "if you know what's good for you, you don't even want to know."

"I don't!" I said. "I hardly even knew him! Golly! I *never* thought he was a crook . . . or anything!"

This cowardly, betraying statement seemed to satisfy both of them. My father marched me toward the door. Just as we reached it, Benny's mother rushed in. I almost did not recognize her. She was wearing a raincoat over a shockingly skimpy costume, her legs in black net hose. Mascara and rouge made her face garish, and she was crying, her tears streaking the cosmetics down her cheeks and chin. For an instant our eyes met. I said nothing. She went by us toward the chief. I heard her weeping tone, the chief's dully angry response. The door closed that world behind us.

In the car, my father drove in angry silence until we had cleared town and were on the highway toward the house. My pulse thudded in my skull. I felt like I might throw up. I was crushed by mortification and guilt. *Nothing* had ever been this bad. I had shamed my parents. I had denied Benny. I was the worst kind of sneak and coward. Making all the guilt feelings worse was the clear realization that I was *glad* Benny had been blamed, because it had cleared me. I loved Benny and he had been my protector. But now he was in Big Trouble and would go to jail, and if it had to be one of us, I was glad it was him and not me. And this made me feel that I was even more a worm.

"Well?" my father said finally, his voice tight. "What do you have to say for yourself?"

"I didn't hook anything," I said abjectly. "I didn't know what was going on."

"Don't give me that stuff," he snapped in a tone he had never used to me before. "Maybe you didn't steal anything, but you would have the next time. What was in your mind, hanging around with a kid like that? Thick as thieves with trash?"

"I didn't know he stole stuff. I didn't even *like* him . . . very much. He just asked me if I wanted to go home with him, and help him with models, so I did. That's *all*."

He thought about that, driving. Finally he said, "Your mother doesn't know about this. She doesn't have to know. Do you realize that something like this would kill her? It would just kill her!"

"I'm sorry," I said, and began crying. "I didn't mean anything—"

"I don't want any of your apologies! If I ever—if I *ever*—get another call from the police about you, son, do you know what's going to happen?"

"What?" I managed, sniffling.

"Nothing," he told me coldly.

I stared at him as he drove, jaw set.

He said, "I won't go in there after you. I won't have the family name disgraced. If you want to be trash, then you can be trash. But I'll never come get you again. If you want to hang around with people like that Harrison kid, then you're telling us, 'Hey, I'm grown up now. I don't need any of you now.' And that's the way it will be. Your mother is a fine woman. Your little sister is a wonderful little girl. You won't drag them down —or me. You'll go to BIS alone."

I was so frightened that my tears stopped. Boys Industrial School was a buzz-word phrase for terror. Only the worst went to BIS. When you went there, it was one step from the penitentiary in Columbus. I saw how seriously I had transgressed, and the chasm at my feet terrified me.

"You'll get no allowance until further notice," he told me.

"You'll clean the barn and you'll do it *right*. No radio for a month. Is that understood?"

"Yessir," I mumbled.

"We'll say nothing about any of this to your mother or Agatha. You understand that, too?"

"Yessir."

He sighed. "I don't know what you had in mind, hanging around with a kid like that. But sometimes God works in mysterious ways. He's had his chance, Squirt. He's lost it. You got another chance. You've got good stuff in you. If you let this be a lesson to you, maybe you can still be the kind of fine young man I know you can be." He glared at me. "Understood?"

I had no idea what precisely I was supposed to understand. "Yessir!" I said.

He breathed deeply again. "All right, then."

The next day I went to school, dreamlike, as if it were a normal day. Of course Benny was not there. I felt his empty desk nearby as if it were filled with fire. I pretended not to notice. But at recess it started to come out.

"Wonder where old Benny is," Jimmy Cantwell said.

"Ain't you heard?" Sheehan said. "He's in jail." He grinned.

"In *jail!*" Everyone was amazed.

"Hooking stuff at a store," Sheehan chuckled. "My old man told me about it. Looks like BIS for sure, boy."

"Good grief," Inright said softly. "I knew he was tough, but—"

"He wasn't so tough," Sheehan sneered. "He just talked tough. All he ever was was a punk, my old man says. BIS is good enough for him. Him and anybody that buddied around with him," he added, looking at me.

Silent, on the edge of being afraid and ashamed, I looked down at my too-small tennis shoes.

"Right, Flatfoot?" Sheehan said.

"Right," I said hoarsely.

"And you got nobody to fight your battles for you anymore," Sheehan went on. "Unless you want to go to BIS with him."

No one spoke. I bit my tongue. It had been one thing to betray Benny with adults. This was even worse. I had no choice because I was afraid . . . afraid.

"BIS," someone said again, reverently.

"And good enough for him," Sheehan said.

"I never thought it would happen," Cantwell said.

"He had it coming," Sheehan said. "He was no good, all blow and no show, just trash. Good riddance to bad rubbish, right, Flatfoot?"

I looked up at him, intent on keeping quiet. The gloating expression drove me over the edge. "You dopus," I said. "You stupid queerbait."

Sheehan's head jerked back. "*What* did you say?"

"Benny is worth a hundred queerbaits like you! If he ever gets out of jail, you'll keep your yap shut!"

Sheehan began dancing around. "You want to make something of it, Flatfoot? You want to put up or shut up? Come on! Come—"

Whether it was conscious or instinctive I will never know. Perhaps I had simply filled up and could not handle any more. Sheehan was still thumbing his nose when I rushed him. My first blow caught him squarely on the mouth and the second caught his right eye. He yelped and staggered backward, falling. I piled on top of him and pounded at his face with both hands.

"I give!" he yelped, covering up. "I give! I give!"

I stopped hitting him, and, shaking all over, got to my feet. Jimmy Cantwell and the others looked like statues with big, round eyes. Sheehan was sniffling blood, trying to wipe some of the mud off his clothes. I faced him with my fists ready. They stung from pounding on him, but in me was a wild, angry elation.

"You hit me when I wasn't looking," he said, dabbing at his nose.

I drew back my right. "You want more?"

"No! No!" He took a step backward.

The class bell sounded. I turned and walked away from them. As Mrs. Broadus started the history lesson, I felt the reaction begin to set in. My arms and legs trembled and I felt sick. But I had faced him. I had faced Bill Sheehan! *You were right, Benny. You were always right. Never let them get set.*

And now, I thought, my troubles at school were over.

I was allowed to think that through the afternoon recess, when we played a little capture the flag without incident, no one even mentioning the earlier scuffle.

When I went back to my desk, however, my tablet had been opened and someone had printed a message to me in red pencil, with a picture of a dagger dripping big drops of red blood. I read it with a new feeling of nausea:

WE WILL GET REVENJE.
YOU WILL DIE.
THE BLOODY HAND GANG

I realized that it was a really stupid note. But my blood chilled.

If school went along badly, and I was haunted by thoughts of Benny Harrison, the work with Skipper provided moments of joy and even elation. He grew prodigiously, and was a large dog already, all legs and big paws, but recognizably a purebred German shepherd—almost. No matter what else happened, I had worked with him every day. He always came now when I whistled for him, and he walked obediently close by my side with or without the leash.

We had even learned a game. I found one of those rubber balls with a bell that rattled loose within its hollow center. Skipper learned to chase it and bring it back to me, tracking it down swiftly and unerringly by its jingling, then homing in on my encouraging voice to return it. I had to be very careful where I threw the ball; once he ran headlong into a corner of the porch, raising a swelling on his left eye. Another time, he collided with a clothesline post. But if I threw it, he galloped after its sound gleefully, full out, trusting that nothing stood in his way. I loved playing the game with him. It made life seem almost normal.

His sense of smell was fantastic, and he was becoming a

good watchdog. At the sound of a stranger approaching, or the person's scent, he often let up a terrific racket. People did not know he was blind and probably harmless. He sounded and looked fierce. It was not until the man from the electric company came that afternoon that I learned Skipper might truly be fierce, and only his obedience averted a possible catastrophe.

We had been playing the game with the ball, and now lay side by side in the shade of the house near the front porch, resting. I was sweaty and itchy from grass, and Skipper panted, his tongue lolling out.

The yellow electric company truck came slowly down the highway. I watched it, idly tickling Skipper's ears, which he liked. When the truck turned into the driveway, Skipper's ears pricked.

"Wonder what he wants," I said.

Skipper licked his mouth and looked directly at the truck as it pulled closer just as if he could see. The engine shut off and a tall man in a pair of dungarees, with a tan cap, got out from behind the wheel. He walked across the driveway toward us. His feet crunched in the gravel. I felt Skipper tense under my hand.

"Hello, son," the man said. "Is your momma inside?"

Skipper's hair stood up. Without warning, his body exploded into action. He crossed the space to the man in a twinkling, and *leaped.*

"What the—!" the man yelled hoarsely, dodging.

Skipper missed him and landed heavily in the gravel. Scrambling up, he wheeled around. I saw his fangs bared. A low, vicious growl came from his throat.

"Call him off, kid!" the man said. His eyes were wide and he was terrified. "Call the—"

Skipper lunged again. The man threw up his arm, and in his hand was some kind of steel-clad booklet for records. I heard Skipper's teeth clash on the metal. The man staggered and fell. Skipper wheeled around, having missed again, and started forward.

"*Skipper!*" I screamed. "Skipper! Heel! *Heel!*"

Skipper stopped dead. The growl coming from his throat sent

chills down my back. The serviceman sprawled, eyes wide with shocked fright.

"Heel, Skipper!" I repeated, and clapped my hands.

Skipper turned and trotted obediently to me. In an instant he was his old self again. I locked my fists in his shaggy hair. "It's okay, Mister! I've got him!"

The serviceman did not move. "Tie him up," he said huskily.

"I've got him!"

"Tie him up! I ain't moving till you tie him up!"

I led Skipper around to the tying post and roped him securely. The man got up, dusted himself off, and went muttering to the front door.

I was amazed. Memory came of what Rudi had once told me about blind animals becoming vicious. If I had not been there, what would Skipper have done?

The thought frightened me. But at the same time I saw that he had obeyed me instantly under the worst possible circumstances. From now on, Skipper would have to be watched more closely. But he had proven to me that he was my dog, under my control. Even as I was shaken, I was proud of him.

On the last day of school we were released early, but a mixup meant a wait of more than an hour for the school buses. It gave me time to do something I had been wanting to do. I hurried every step of the way, and required less than ten minutes, mostly running, to cross the river and walk up the street, breathing hard, to Benny Harrison's house.

The porch swing on the porch was empty and the house looked deserted. Nevertheless, I went to the door and rapped loudly on it. I heard nothing. I was about to turn away when the door opened. Benny's mother, with a robe wrapped around her, looked out at me.

"Hullo, Mrs. Harrison," I said. "I'm Benny's friend. Remember?"

"Why, yes," she said. She managed a wan smile. "Hello."

"I, uh, was going by, and I, uh, thought I would say hello."

"That was nice of you . . . Danny, isn't it?" She wiped her

eyes with the backs of her hands as if she had been sleeping. Or crying. "Would you like to come in?"

I knew I didn't have much time, but I had to know. I went in and sat on the couch in the wrecked living room. She offered cookies. I refused.

"Are you all right, Danny?" she asked finally. "You look so pale."

"Mrs. Harrison, how's Benny? What's happened to him?"

Her lips set. "Why, Danny, I imagine he's just fine. And he's now at Boys Industrial School."

It was the worst. I stared at her.

"He's doing just fine," she told me with a hectic, false smile. "He mentioned you just last weekend."

"How long did he—I mean, how long is he going to be there, Mrs. Harrison?"

"Well, the rest of this school year, then through the summer."

"You mean he'll be coming back to our school in the fall?"

"No. When Benny gets out, Danny, we'll . . . move somewhere else."

"Is he really all right, Mrs. Harrison? Is he *really?*"

"Why, yes," she told me. "He has regular classes, and they also have nice things like shop, where a young boy can begin learning a trade. I think he's doing just wonderfully, Danny."

"Will you tell him I came by?" I asked.

"Why, of course."

"And—and would you tell him I did what he taught me? To Bill Sheehan?"

She frowned. "To Bill Sheehan? Will he understand that?"

"Yessum. He will."

"All right, Danny. It was very sweet of you to come by."

She walked with me to the door. As I started out, she hugged me. I leaned close to her and kissed her cheek. Her breath caught and tears started in her eyes. She did not speak. I hurried down the steps and away from the house, and when I looked back from the corner, she was still standing in the doorway. She waved. I waved back.

Hurrying across the bridge again, I was crossing Main Street when the two truckloads of prisoners pulled up in front of the

Harmon Ice Company. The gates of the front truck let down, and a half dozen of the prisoners climbed out, four guards with them. Mr. Harmon came out of the ice company, handed out some ice tongs, and opened the heavy doors of the cooler building.

The prisoners with the tongs trooped into the building. Harmon, a heavyset man with a shaggy shelf of eyebrows, stood by glaring. In a moment the first prisoner came back out carrying a fifty-pound cake of ice. As he hefted it into the back of the truck, a second prisoner came out with another cake. He proceeded to the truck as the third prisoner came out.

The third prisoner stumbled slightly coming out of the building. The heavy cake of ice fell from the tongs, hitting Harmon's leg. Harmon danced back, his face contorting. He shoved the prisoner and said something. The prisoner, a thin man with a scarred face, dropped his tongs and pushed Harmon. Harmon snatched another pair of tongs off the wall and drew them back as if to strike. Two of the soldiers rushed over and grabbed both men. I saw angry words being exchanged. Harmon got one arm loose and made a slashing gesture in the air. The soldiers gave orders. The prisoners were all hustled back into the truck.

As the truck engines were started, a man ran from the service station next to the ice company. He had a rifle or shotgun in his hands. I saw another man come out of the barbershop across the street, and although he was not armed, his anger was clear. The trucks lurched into motion and lumbered down the street, getting out of there.

For a moment I did not move. It had been a very near thing. If the soldiers had not moved swiftly, blood would have been spilled. For my father, I thought, this could only mean more trouble.

10

As a result of the incident on Harmony's Main Street, a meeting was held in our living room the following evening. Colonel Thatcher was there, along with Mr. Sheehan and two men I had not seen before: Mayor Gump and Sheriff Lockwood. The atmosphere, even as my mother served iced tea and cookies, was tense. The colonel could not sit still and kept prowling the room. Mr. Sheehan sat with fat legs spread, fanning himself with a magazine. Gump was an older man, wizened, owner of a hardware store; he looked permanently soured on the world and did not even seem to like my mother's iced tea as he sipped it. The sheriff, in a tan-and-gray uniform, sat stolidly, unhappy, in my father's favorite chair while my father stood by the mantel.

At the dining room table, pretending to read, I was able to see and hear everything.

"We appreciate your offering your house," the colonel said. "Have a meeting in town and it looks like an emergency. People at the camp would talk." He glowered at my father. "But obviously we have a problem."

My father frowned. "The guards' reports are clear. It was a minor incident. Nothing serious happened."

"I was on the street within seconds," Sheehan retorted. "I saw no less than three of our businessmen with guns. I tell you, Davidson, we came within a hair's-breadth of tragedy. A hair's-breadth!"

My father looked pale and drawn. "That may be. But it was not any fault of the prisoners."

"People don't like it," Mayor Gump said shrilly. "They're scared. Want them Germans out of here."

"They're not likely to be out of the area," my father replied. "They're needed to work the farms."

"Ought to have more guards. Keep 'em out of our town. Don't want 'em running wild in our town."

"They're not running wild," my father said patiently. "The trucks stopped to pick up some ice. One of the prisoners dropped a piece of ice, hitting Mr. Harmon. He—"

"We all know what happened, Davidson," the colonel broke in. "It was a mistake for those trucks to be in town."

"Possibly," my father conceded. "However, we need to remember that prisoners did not run wild. They did not threaten Harmony. They were never out of control. If anyone caused trouble, it was Mr. Harmon, not our people."

"I think Harmon's reaction was understandable," Sheehan said. "We've all been tense. It isn't normal, having dangerous people running around. Allowances have to be made."

"Dangerous people were not running around," my father said. His face was pink, the way it got when he was angry. "The prisoners were following orders and under guard."

"Whose side are you on, anyway?" Mayor Gump shrilled.

"There *aren't* any sides."

"You don't think them Germans are the enemy?"

Before my father could reply, Sheehan added, "What you sometimes seem to forget, George, is just what the mayor is reminding you. Those Germans may be prisoners, but they're still soldiers of the Third Reich. Under different circumstances they would still be over on the other side, killing our boys."

"But that's not the circumstances we have," my father retorted. "Except for a few minor incidents, we've been very, very lucky. The prisoners have been extraordinarily well behaved. Our security is good."

"What about Grove City?" Mayor Gump snapped.

"That was not an escape."

"What about last week?"

My father's flush deepened. "Those two men were picked up within an hour. There was absolutely no harm done."

"That may be," Sheehan said. "And you know my position. The camp is good for business. We need to keep it if we possibly can. But between ourselves we have to face facts. Potentially, those men are all dangerous. Given the chance, they would break out, arm themselves, and take over this entire area. In their circumstances, I would be trying to figure out ways to do the same thing."

"Our security is excellent," my father retorted. "We're making a mountain out of a molehill."

Sheriff Lockwood stirred. "It won't be a molehill if people start shooting."

"Then it's for you and the police to make sure the people don't start it," my father snapped.

"Keep them out of our town!" Mayor Gump said.

"Gentlemen," Colonel Thatcher broke in, "it won't accomplish anything to argue. What we face here is a situation that must be dealt with firmly and openly. The populace must be reassured. The prisoners must be forced to see that they are in no position to strike back, whatever the provocation. Some of our procedures need to be tightened. In the first place, Mr. Mayor, I am issuing a directive that trucks bearing prisoners will no longer stop in, or even drive through, your community."

"And we don't need them soldiers, either," Gump said. "I'm as patriotic as the next man, but they cause trouble, standing around, making remarks at the womenfolk. We don't have that kind of a town here."

The colonel's face hardened. "I will not put Harmony off limits to our men. However, I will issue a letter outlining the need for the strictest decorum."

The mayor muttered and no one else spoke. The colonel

paced to the front windows, looked out at the night, and turned back. "As to the prisoners involved in the incident of yesterday, disciplinary action will be taken."

My father reacted as if he had been slapped. "Like what?"

"Extra work details. Suspension of allowance for cigarettes and other personal needs until further notice."

"Is that fair?"

"It's necessary. The disciplinary action will serve to dampen any ideas any of the rest of them might have that they can get away with anything. Face it, Davidson: no matter how closely we guard those men, they will come in contact with locals when working outside the camp. Remarks will be made. That's human nature. The men have to know without doubt that any response on their part will result in punishment."

Sheehan said, "We can make sure the paper has a story on that. It ought to make people feel a little better."

"All guards," the colonel added, "will be issued additional instructions. They will tolerate *no* misbehavior by any prisoner. If necessary to prevent a disturbance, they will shoot to kill."

"Kill a few of 'em," Mayor Gump said, "and it ought to straighten the rest of 'em out!"

Sheehan, like my father, had gone slightly pale. "Well, now, we don't want any violence. That's what all of us are trying to prevent, here."

Colonel Thatcher turned to my father. "I expect you to make sure the civilians understand the new orders also. They've been armed from the start, but I have noticed astonishing laxity on the part of some of them. I expect them to wear or carry their weapons at all times they are on duty. It would not hurt if you followed those orders yourself. When you're out in the compound, I want to see you wearing your sidearm."

My father's face twisted. "Everything has gone far more smoothly than any of us had any right to hope," he said. "One minor incident—"

"An incident can become an epidemic, Davidson," the colonel said. "That's why we have to take action at once."

"I can't predict how everyone will react to this, Colonel.

Some of our new civilians—none of us knows them well. They might seize on an excuse. The prisoners—"

"It seems to me, Davidson, that if you spent more time worrying about the heart of your responsibilities—security—and less in being a bleeding heart on behalf of enemy soldiers, we would all be a lot better off."

There was an instant of total silence. I saw my father's stricken expression—the look of shock that crossed Sheehan's face. The colonel seemed oblivious to his own cruelty. "I hope word of our sterner measures, Mr. Mayor, will be carried in the newspaper." He glanced at Sheehan. "You can be sure I will make our position clear when I speak next week to the Chamber of Commerce. In the meantime, I think it is incumbent on law officials to issue similar statements emphasizing the harsh action that will be taken if any civilian causes trouble."

"I'll see the chief," Sheriff Lockwood said. "We'll get out a statement of our own."

"Good." The colonel looked around. "Anything further?"

My father started to speak, seemed to think better of it, then slowly shook his head as he again changed his mind. "We're overreacting," he said.

Everyone looked at him.

"By doing all this," he told them, "you're making it seem that a lot more happened than did happen." He looked at the colonel. "You're going to crowd the men until something really serious happens."

"Davidson," Colonel Thatcher said heavily, "each of us has his duty. It was a blow to me when I was given this assignment. By background and inclination I should be a combat soldier. But this is my duty as assigned and I intend to carry it out to the best of my ability. I think that's what each of us must do. Your job is to carry out my orders unquestioningly. We don't need second-guessers here."

My father met his eyes. There was another silence. It was Sheehan who broke it with a sigh as he got to his feet. "Well, gentlemen, I think that covers it."

There was some hand-shaking and general comment and

then they all went out to their cars. Headlights flared over the front of the house as they backed out onto the road, leaving one by one. My father stood on the porch, watching them go. My mother remained in the kitchen. I did not know how much she might have heard.

I went to the front door and met him coming back in as the last car droned into the night. His eyes in an unguarded moment were empty and remote. Then he seemed to see me standing there, watching. "Well, Squirt," he said.

My mother came in from the kitchen. Her face said she had heard enough. "What do you think?"

He shook his head. "I think it's a mistake. An awful mistake."

"Why didn't you make them not do it?" I demanded.

"How could I?" he shot back.

"Danny," my mother said with soft warning.

But I was not to be turned. "You're in charge of the guards! You could have told the colonel you wouldn't do it! Those guys aren't going to hurt folks! They're *tired,* a lot of them, and homesick. And scared. Those people in town are just dummies, and the colonel is a mean old—old *turd."*

"Danny!" my mother repeated in quite a different tone.

My father reached out and tousled my hair. "When you're a man, Squirt, you follow orders. Sometimes—"

"When you know the orders are wrong? That's not being a man! That's being a coward!"

He stiffened. "Go to your room."

"Dad, I—"

"I said go to your room! I've taken all I'm going to take tonight and I'm not taking it from a boy who doesn't know what he's talking about!"

"Dad—"

"Go!"

He had betrayed me. None of us—even my friend Rudi—could count on him for anything. And now if worse things happened, *he* would be as much a cause as anyone. I ran from the room so they would not see my tears.

"You shouldn't have shouted at him," I heard my mother say behind me.

"Are you going to get on me too?" my father shot back.

I closed the door of my room, then, and could hear only the murmur of their voices. Skipper moved next to me, tail thumping, and I petted him. I sat on the side of the bed, sniffling.

The door of the room opened behind me. I thought it was one of my parents, but when I turned I was surprised to see Aggie, in her long nightdress, slipping into the room. She closed the door behind her and padded barefoot to my side. She climbed up onto the bed and put a little arm around me.

"That's awright, Danny," she said comfortingly.

"You're supposed to be asleep," I growled.

"I heard all the loud voices so I couldn't. Do you think they're gonna shoot all the Germans like that nice man that comes and talks to you about Skip?"

"I don't know," I told her. "What do I care?"

"Danny, I'm sorry about Benny Harrison."

"Yeah." I was close to crying again.

"Do you think he'll ever come back to school?"

"No. When he gets out, he'll move away."

"Then I guess Bill Sheehan will beat up on you every day, huh?"

"What do you know?" I snarled.

She patted me some more, swinging her legs. "It's all right, Danny. Skipper will be all right and they won't kill the nice man for being a German and you'll get the weeds all out of the garden, I promise. I'll help you. I will."

"Sure," I said.

"Have I made you feel all nice and better?" she asked.

"Yes, Aggie. You've made me feel a lot better. Thank you."

"Okay," she sighed cheerfully, hopping off the bed. She padded back to the door, opened it, whisked out, and closed it behind her.

After sitting a few more minutes, I got up and undressed for bed. My mother and father were still talking quietly in the living room. I wondered what they were discussing now. I wished we could move back to Columbus.

The door opened again shortly after I had stretched out. It was Aggie again, this time bagging along one of her cats, now practically as big as she was. It was the darker one named Christopher.

She swung Christopher up onto my chest. The cat dug in his claws to hang on.

"Ouch!"

"Here you are, Danny," Aggie whispered. "You can have Christopher tonight. That'll make you feel even more better."

Before I could protest, she was gone again. Skipper smelled the cat and growled a little, although frequently the cats played all over him, roughhousing, and he never so much as raised an eyelid. Christopher yawned, showing bright pink gums and an incredible array of little teeth, then snuggled down on top of me and began to purr. I rubbed him gently behind the ears and thought about the summer that lay before us. It was going to be lonely without Benny. I could not count on my father. Whatever I did, I was going to have to do on my own.

For some reason, it was in this context that I thought again of that ghastly pipe in the bank of the creek. *Maybe you can't do much about most things,* I thought. *But you can do something about that.*

And if I got killed, I thought spitefully, they would all be really sorry, and it would serve them right!

All right, then, I told myself, in the morning I'll explore it. All the way.

It did not seem very scary in the safety of my bed.

In the morning, standing again in the creek mud and looking up at the pipe, it was quite a different matter. My ball of string and flashlight in hand, I began again to think of all the other things I might be doing. One of our sugar ration coupons was due to be honored today, and I knew my mother would be making cookies before many hours passed. It seemed important that I should be on hand to taste some of the first ones out of the oven to tell her they were all right. There was always the garden. And Skipper had looked distinctly sad when I went off and left him. I was in the middle of a book, *A Yank in the*

RAF, full of great adventures in P-38s, and I could be reading that.

Somehow, however, completing this adventure in the tunnel seemed more important today. I was scared of Bill Sheehan, and even of Inright. Benny Harrison was gone. My father was scared of Colonel Thatcher . . . and was not the man I had always imagined. If I couldn't even get up the nerve to walk through this dumb old *pipe,* what was there left for me?

Thus bolstered, I climbed into the tunnel. I started in bravely enough, but as the cool vapors closed around me, my resolve began to slip away. I kept going; today a steady stream of water rippled along the lowest curved portion, and I had to walk astraddle, moving along like some kind of subterranean crab. My flashlight batteries were already going down, casting a weak yellow light, which did not reassure me. I gritted my teeth and told myself I would *not* look back to the beautiful outside world.

When I reached the beginning of the long curve in the tunnel, I went right on, carefully playing out my depleting ball of twine. Soon I reached the point where my nerves had last failed me; ahead I could again hear the distant rumble. I paused, sweating, and thought about turning back. *You've come this far. Keep going!*

Gulping a breath, I did so.

The air became danker and heavier as I proceeded. The rumble grew louder, a steady throbbing note that seemed to vibrate the grayish walls of the tunnel. I began to think it was machinery of some kind, and felt a little better.

At this point the dwindling ball of string in my hand became a few lose strands. I stopped and shone my flashlight down, and calculated. I could go only a few more feet before it ran out. But I told myself there was no problem with this because I had not encountered any branches that might get me lost. I went on, reached the end of the string, let it drop, and crabbed ahead.

I had not gone more than another twenty paces when the tunnel branched into three passageways.

This was a real problem. I must *not* get myself confused. I thought about it. It was another wonderful chance to go back. But if I went back, I was defeated again. I decided to bear right at every branch, and then I could always get back by bearing left.

Shaking my flashlight to make it momentarily a little brighter, I waddled into the righthand tunnel.

The stream of water in this branch was lighter, hardly more than a trickle. I was sweating heavily as I moved along. How long *was* this tunnel?

The rumbling was louder. With it beating in my eardrums, I came to another branching, this time into four more tunnels. Again I took the rightmost one. But I had gone only a few steps when abruptly the tunnel became smaller, hardly more than five feet in diameter now, forcing me to bend over sharply at the waist to keep going.

I crabbed along, really getting upset now. If the pipe got any smaller, I would have no choice but to turn back. I shone the flashlight anxiously ahead—and saw a dead end.

There was nothing but solid rock wall. The tunnel simply stopped. I played the light on the ceiling and saw that it extended upward, but whatever was above was only blackness, and no way to get up there to explore further.

I turned and backtracked. At the first intersection I turned to the right and proceeded again. The tunnel again became smaller. *This was not right if I was going back outside.*

I stopped and thought about it, my heartbeat louder than the rumbling in the walls. Of course it was not right. I had been backtracking, and should not have turned right. I should have turned left. I went back to the junction. In the sprayed light of the dying flashlight, all four tunnels looked identical. *Be calm, be calm,* I told myself. I came out of *there* . . . and I came in *here* . . . so the tunnel back must be *that* one.

The new tunnel narrowed abruptly just like the other ones. Which meant I was wrong again.

By this time, panic was taking over. Had I made two right turns in two sets of tunnels, or one right turn and one wrong one? And which set was I in now? Should I go back or keep on? If I went back, which way should I turn next? I began breathing hard, hyperventilating and getting dizzy. I told myself I was every kind of dopus, and then some.

But what to do?

I decided grimly to keep going. If this tunnel, too, dead-ended, then perhaps all of them did except the one that led back home. I would just keep going until I either found my way out or reached a dead end.

Or died, the thought came wildly.

Lecturing myself to be calm, which was now impossible, I continued. The tunnel curved again. I went on. The flashlight was now on its last legs and I was muttering prayers. Suddenly I turned the corner and up ahead was something that startled and hurt my eyes—distant light!

I ran, splashing in the thin stream of water. I reached a narrow shaft which marked the end of this tunnel, like the one at the end of the earlier one. But here the shaft went up to a beautiful, wonderful, thrilling patch of blinding bright sky. And on the wall, leading up to a distant metal grating of some kind, was a steel ladder.

I climbed it with frantic speed. Reaching the heavy metal grate, I tried to see out. I could not see anything but the edge of something big and metal against the summer sky. It had to be the machinery that filled everything with its rumble. I caught a breath of fresher air mixed with oily fumes, and heaved on the grating. It did not want to budge. Desperation gave me strength. Balling myself on the top rung on the metal ladder, I heaved with all the strength left in me.

The grating popped out of its rusty socket, showering me with fragments and dirt. I popped my head up, gulping the blessed free air.

The machine was huge, some kind of generator. It hulked beside an old brick wall of a tall building which looked somehow familiar. Turning my head, I saw that I had come out of a manhole at the edge of a sprawling paved courtyard with another old brick building about thirty yards away, and newer frame barracks to my immediate left and right. The courtyard was filled with men in dark fatigue clothing. German prisoners.

Before I could recover my surprise at coming up inside the

camp, some of the men nearest me turned and saw me. Their expressions went quickly from surprise to shock to something else—fear. Several of them ran toward me—grabbed my arms—helped me climb out to solid earth.

"Gosh, fellows, thanks a lot!" I gasped. "I—"

Someone put a rough hand over my mouth, closing off my words. Strong hands lifted me and propelled me swiftly across a blurred terrain. Other prisoners were running. They got me to the door of a barracks and rushed me inside. I was tossed down rudely on the nearest of dozens of cots lining the barren walls. The door slammed, then reopened again as more Germans rushed in. I struggled, but the man holding me kept his hand over my mouth. All my old fears rioted. The prisoners had taken a prisoner.

The Germans—more than a dozen of them—babbled excitedly at each other in their own tongue. Two of them ran back outside. I stopped struggling, and my captor, a big man with a beard, held me in a fierce grip.

It was definitely a barracks for the prisoners: rows of cots on either long wall comprised the only furnishings. The bare wood floor gleamed. A small footlocker was arranged at the foot of each cot, but there were no other signs of places for personal effects. Sunlight was bright against the tall, bare windows. The Germans stared at me, their eyes wide with surprise and shock and that other element I had seen earlier—simple fear.

The door swung open again and about a dozen new prisoners boiled in. One of them was older than any of the others, evidently a senior officer. He took one look at me as if he was going to have a stroke, then unleashed a barrage of German at my captor. They had a brief, guttural conversation with some of the others joining in. I figured they were going to tear me limb from limb.

The officer—if that was what he was—turned to one of the men and issued some orders. That man, a lank blond of perhaps twenty, came over and stiffly addressed me:

"What haf you done to come into zis place?"

"I was exploring the tunnel!" I said the moment my captor

removed his hand from my mouth. "I didn't know where I was coming up! Honest!"

The soldier repeated my words in German, and the officer barked something in reply. The soldier turned to me again. "How many ozzers know of zis tunnel?"

"Nobody!" I said. Then I thought, *Oh, God, if they know I'm alone, they will kill me.* "Just me and my pals," I added. "And if I don't get right back home, of course they'll send the Army."

There was another heated exchange in German. One of the others added something and the officer barked an order that silenced him. If there was an overwhelming impression, it was that these men were terrified. I did not know what that meant for me.

The door opened again. The first prisoner who had gone out came back in, followed by a familiar figure. My relief was like a hot flash. "Rudi!" I cried. "Tell these guys to lemme alone!"

Rudi, ashen, hurried over. The older man snapped something. Rudi jerked to attention and answered. They had a sharp exchange. Rudi saluted and hurried to me. He knelt and held my hand. "Be calm, Danny." He looked far from calm. "What is this thing you have done? You came out of the *sewer?*"

"I was exploring, Rudi, honest! I didn't know where I was going! I ran out of string and then the tunnels forked and I got mixed up and my dumb flashlight was going dead and I seen this manhole and I climbed up, but I didn't mean to bother anybody, *really!*"

Rudi patted my hand and turned to the officer, explaining in German. The officer barked something back, clearly worried.

Rudi turned back to me. "How many others know of the sewer?"

"Nobody! I came on it by accident, and I was just exploring —I got mixed up—"

Rudi turned and reported this to the officer. The officer smacked his own forehead with the palm of his hand, rolled his eyes toward heaven, and strode up and down the barracks in silence.

Rudi turned back to me. "This is a very dangerous thing you have done."

"I knew that when I got lost!"

He registered surprise. "Not for you. For *us*."

"Huh?"

"You have discovered the sewer which leads out of the camp."

I tumbled. "It's your escape hatch!" I whispered. "Oh, Rudi, listen! I'll never tell! I won't! You guys want to escape, just let me go and I'll *never* tell! I—"

"Escape?" Rudi said. "Do you think we are mad?"

"But if you've got the tunnel—"

He touched my lips with his fingertip. "I will explain. We found this sewer—the gratings—almost at once. They had been . . . what is the word . . . overlooked. But *we* do not want to escape. In France or Africa? Yes. It would be our duty to try to escape. Even in England, yes. But here? In America? Where would we go? *Mein Gott!* Those people in the town would kill us!"

"Then you don't *care* that I found my way in!" I gasped in relief.

"We could not tell your colonel what we had found," Rudi told me. "He would have said we were trying to escape. So we have told no one. No one must know. Not all of us inside know. A few idiots might even try to use the sewer, and bring down trouble on all the rest of us."

"But why didn't you tell the colonel?"

"He would have said it was a plot. There might have been reprisals." Rudi grimaced. "No. Far better to *pretend* we do not know."

I began to understand. They were in the middle of an insane game here. They really did want to stay in the camp and cause no trouble, just as my father had said earlier. And they were so frightened—those who knew—that they couldn't even admit knowledge for fear of what it might bring.

And I had poked my head up right in the middle of their secret.

The officer said something to Rudi. Rudi replied. The officer groaned and waved his arms and began pacing again. Rudi grimaced. "You present us a problem, Danny."

"Just let me get out of here," I said. "Just tell me which way to go. I'll never tell *anyone*. I promise!"

Rudi turned back to the officer and they had another exchange. One or two of the other men joined in, but the officer snapped an order and they shut up, stony-faced.

Rudi lifted me down out of the other man's arms. "We are going to try to get you back to the sewer. I will take you back to the creek. You must promise never to tell anyone, or we would be in grave trouble."

"I promise, Rudi! I do!"

Rudi said something to the officer. The officer gave a long speech to all the men in German. There were some questions. Evidently the orders were amended. Some of the men worriedly hurried out. I realized that a conspiratorial air had filled the barracks.

Rudi took my hand and led me to the door. Another man held it cracked. Others stood anxiously at the windows.

Out on the parade ground, or whatever it might be called, several of the men who had been in the barracks were now standing on the pavement well away from the barracks, waving their arms and yelling at one another. To my astonishment, I saw one of them push another. The two men tangled, evidently fighting, and went to the pavement. Some of the others began yelling. From around the corners of buildings ran some civilian and army guards to intervene.

At this moment I saw no more, because Rudi had grabbed my arm and propelled me out the door. With others running with us, we dashed into the shadows of the brick building. Some of the men hauled the grating back. Rudi climbed down inside. Others thrust me after him. He caught me and went down the metal grating with me pressed against his chest.

He had a flashlight from somewhere. My own had been lost, and his was much better anyway. He ran, dragging me, and went through the maze like it was a straight line. Minutes later, breathing hard, he brought me to the tranquil setting where the pipe disgorged into our creek.

He knelt in the water, handing me down. "You must never do this again," he said severely. He was badly out of breath.

"I never will!" I promised.

With a final hard look, he turned and raced back into the sewer. I listened to his footsteps, receding and finally vanishing entirely.

I looked around the creek. A bird sang. The sky had puffy clouds in it. I could hardly believe it. The world, I thought, was truly crazy.

11

For a number of days things were very quiet on the farm. I worked every morning in the garden, hoeing around the sprouting beans, lettuce, radishes, potatoes, spinach, and corn. There was no rain, and I hauled our old hose out of the barn, hooked it up, and watered the hard-cracked earth in the garden plot. I kept my mouth shut about my sewer adventure.

"I tell you one thing," my mother said one morning when I went out with my dog, having him heel through the kitchen. "That animal thinks the sun rises and sets with you."

"Sure he does," I told her. "He ought to. I'm his best pal."

I was trying to teach Skipper "right" and "left" as commands in his walking, and progress was slow. Whenever I sensed that he was losing patience with me, or vice versa, we wrestled. The signal for that game was for me to grab him around the neck and tumble to the grass. He tried to get free. I held on. He shook and dragged me around. When I slipped loose, he piled on top of me, mauling me with his big, lethal, slobbering teeth. Every once in a while he forgot himself and hurt me a little, although he never broke the skin. On those occasions I popped him on the nose with my fist, lightly, and he looked stunned and repentant. Then I had to love him for five minutes before he got over his feelings being hurt.

We liked to take walks. Usually we went down the hill to the creek and the heavy brush. By the time we got there, because the weather was now humid and very warm, Skipper drank from the creek until his belly hung down. I always wondered why he liked the creek water better than the water in his pan until one day I lay on the mossy bank and tried it myself. It was spring-cold, making your teeth ache, and tasted brightly of iron. I had never tasted anything so delicious. Sometimes I lay very still after I had drunk, and the minnows and tadpoles would swim back into view where my initial movement had frightened them.

If there was a bane to Skipper's existence, it was Aggie's pair of cats. Many times when he was asleep in the shade beside the house they crept up and cuddled beside him, kneading his fur with their claws as if he were their mother. He would wriggle and yawn but never snap. If a fly made one of his ears twitch, both cats would be on him in an instant, wanting to play with his ears. Both cats thought his food was far better than theirs, and sneaked in beside him to steal some of his supper unless I watched closely. I always expected one of them to vanish down Skipper's gullet as he hawked in his food in the evening, but they nonchalantly kept their noses in the bowl right with him until his big tongue, searching for a final morsel, staggered them out of the way.

At night when I let Skipper out for a final few moments, Christopher especially liked to frighten him. The cat would come skulking around the porch and lie very still, a shadow, while poor Skipper lumbered into the grass to relieve himself. Just when Skipper appeared the most relaxed, Christopher would dart through the darkness and stab with a claw at one of his legs. Skipper would yelp and jump two feet straight into the air. It got to the point where Skipper would not go out without me beside him to protect him. Aggie thought it was very funny.

"One of these days," I growled, "Skipper will forget his manners and bite that cat in two."

"*Skipper?*" Aggie trilled. She clapped her hands with delight. "Oh, Danny! Don't be so *silly!*"

He had become a good watchdog. Night or day—because they were the same to him—any alien sound set off his barking. When we had a telephone installed—the first we had ever had—I had to take him to the barn before the serviceman would get out of his truck. It awed me sometimes that my blind Skipper could so frighten strangers. With us he was the most docile, loving creature imaginable.

One morning, after a brief, intense rainstorm had piled new debris in the creek below the house, a handful of prisoners came over to clear it and prevent flooding upstream. Rudi was among them. Although the guards watched us closely, with a sullen intensity, we managed a few minutes of talk during the rest period.

"A dog has a great heart," Rudi told me. "Great. Deep. But not wide. A dog like this one loves a few. Others are all the same to him. They are not you. Therefore they are enemy."

"You don't think he would bite anybody, do you?"

Rudi looked surprised. "Of course he would bite somebody! Let someone try to harm you, and give him a chance to find them with his teeth!"

"I hope that never happens. Boy! My parents would make me get rid of him for sure then!"

"Does he always obey your commands?"

"Yes."

"Without delay?"

"Yes."

"Then, if you watch over him, a time may never come for him to get into trouble."

"Are you okay?" I asked, abruptly changing the subject.

"Me?" He seemed surprised. "Yes."

"Are they feeding you bread and water over there, or what?"

His rare grin came, showing bad teeth. "Your father is in charge, *ja?* He would feed us bread and water?"

"The colonel would. Especially if he knew about that tunnel, boy!"

"Oh, yes. The colonel. But he does not know. You have been silent."

"If you ask me, they oughtta send the colonel to fight the Japs."

"I am sure many would be pleased at that."

"My dad is scared of him," I said.

"Of the colonel? He is a very . . . formidable man."

"I think he's a dopus. When I grow up, I'm not going to be scared of *anybody*."

"I hope that is true, Danny."

"I won't be like my *dad,* anyway."

Rudi's face lengthened. "You must never speak disrespectfully of your father."

"But he lets the colonel do anything he *wants!*"

"The colonel is the commandant. Your father is powerless."

"He's as bad as Bill Sheehan's dad. Just because you're prisoners—"

"You will not speak disrespectfully of your father!" Rudi snapped.

I stared, shocked by the sudden harsh tone of his voice. Instantly the hardness vanished from his eyes and he smiled. "It is not the way of things."

"Even if he's wrong?"

"Especially if he is wrong, he needs your support. If a father cannot have the support of his own sons, what does he have left? Eh?"

"Did you ever try to escape?" I asked.

"No."

"There! I told you! They act like you're *criminals!* I—"

"Danny, some of my countrymen would escape. Yes. They would. Some are hard. They say, 'This is enemy land.' They would be dangerous. The colonel and your father are not entirely wrong if they are stern."

I looked around at the Germans scattered along the creek bank. "Not any of *these* guys, though!"

"Even some of these. Yes."

I met his eyes. "They don't *look* mean."

"It is not a question of meanness. It is a matter of war."

"I'll be glad when this dumb war is over! I don't even understand it very well!"

His smile returned. "We are alike, then."

"What are you going to do when it's over?"

"I hope . . . go home."

"To Germany?"

"*Ja.*"

"What will you do?"

"Open my business again. Train dogs to obey. Try to make them well if they are sick."

"I don't know what I'm going to do," I said. "All I know how to do is pull weeds and read and do models."

"Then perhaps you will be an engineer."

"I don't think so. That sounds hard."

He reached into his pants pocket and took something out. "I have something for you." He unrolled a three-foot leather leash made of several strands of leather beautifully braided. One end formed a hand loop, and on the other was a metal snapper for the collar.

"Wow!" I moved it in my hands, feeling its oily softness. "Where did you get this?"

"I made it. The snap, from a broken canteen. The leather, I peeled from a belt." He grinned and raised his floppy shirt to reveal a length of rope knotted around his waist to hold up his baggy pants. "See?"

"It's just beautiful," I told him. "I never saw such a beautiful leash."

"It is strong," he told me. "It will never break." Absently he patted his upper left shirt pocket. Almost simultaneously the guards blew their whistles and it was time to resume work.

"Thank you very, very much," I said.

Rudi made a gesture. "Nothing." He got to his feet and joined the others.

They worked through the afternoon at the creek, and although we did not get a chance to visit again, I watched from a distance as I worked in the garden. On two other occasions I saw Rudi forgetfully pat his shirt pocket. Only when I then saw him speak to another prisoner, and take a cigarette from him, did I understand. He was out of cigarettes.

This, I thought, was something I could do for *him*.

That Saturday when we all went into town to the grocery, I had my life's savings, almost a dollar, in my pocket. Sometimes I walked from the grocery while my parents shopped and visited the drugstore to look at models or comic books. This time when I walked into the drugstore, however, I was in a sweat.

No one was on the side where they sold most of their goods, but the owner, Mr. Epperman, was behind the soda fountain. I marched up to the counter and waited for him to cross the store to me and peer over the glass counter stacked high on top with all manner of items. "Yes, sonny?"

"Pack of Pall Malls, please," I said.

"You've got to be kidding," he told me.

"My dad is outside," I said. "He doesn't want to come in. He hurt his foot."

"Well, sonny, we don't sell fags to children. So tell your daddy I'm sorry, but he'll have to come in his own self."

"Just one pack!"

"No!"

"He's sure gonna be mad," I said, skulking to the rack where they had the model planes.

"No opening those boxes to look at the plans!" he called after me.

I stood at the rack looking at the colorful cardboard boxes. There was a Spitfire like I had made, and also Stukas, Junkers, P-40s and other Lockheeds, Grummans, and a dumb old Piper. I hardly noticed them. I was determined to repay Rudi's kindness. There was only one way.

Picking out a P-40 model, I went back to the high counter. Mr. Epperman looked over his glasses at me. "What do you want this time? A cigar?"

"Here," I muttered, handing up the model.

"Thirteen cents," he said.

I handed him a quarter.

He turned to the register.

I slipped a pack of Camels off the counter and into my pocket.

Mr. Epperman handed me my change and my model. "There you go."

"Thanks," I said, starting for the door.

"Hey, sonny?" he called.

Oh, God, I thought. *Caught!* I looked back. "Yessir?"

"Sure you don't want to try for a beer?" he asked, and cackled.

It was a heady feeling, being a thief. I got the cigarettes home and hid them in my desk. A day or two later, I saw the prisoners working in a field just up the road. Hiding the pack in my pants, I hiked up there and sure enough, Rudi was in the gang. I stood at the fence, watching. When a break came, he limped over to me.

"Hello!" he said. "It is hot." He wiped his face on a rag.

"I got something for you," I said.

"Oh?"

I dug out the cigarettes.

He took the pack, examined it, and looked gravely at me. "Where did you get these?"

"I bought 'em."

"They would sell to one so young?"

"Well, I know the man at the store."

"You are not in trouble over this?"

"No! Why should I be in trouble? Go ahead. Smoke one!"

Rudi looked again at the pack and carefully put it in his shirt pocket. "I will not smoke one today. I will smoke one tomorrow," he said soberly. He extended his hand. "Thank you."

I shook his hand. "What are friends for?" I asked.

We had more heavy rains over the next week, and north of Columbus there was some flooding. When we went to the grocery that weekend, I was startled to see the Big Walnut running bank-full, carrying limbs and other debris. My father said the rain had let up just in time to prevent flooding south of Columbus, too. But Sunday was sunny and warm, and on Monday, when I was working in the garden, Bill Sheehan and Phil In-right pedaled up on their bikes.

"Hey, Flatfoot," Sheehan said as they dismounted in the driveway.

"Hey yourself," I said.

"So this is where he lives, huh?" Inright said.

"Yep," Sheehan said as if I weren't there. "He's got a real little room with some crummy models in it."

"I'd like to see that," Inright said.

I stood facing them, my hands on my hips.

"So you want to go riding with us?" Sheehan asked.

"I don't have a bike," I said.

Sheehan patted the handlebars of his bike, which was a red Fleetwing, a fancy one with a front light on the fender, a rack, a can between the bars for a horn, white sidewall tires, and two mirrors canted outward at a thirty-degree angle. Inright's bike, older, was a Roadmaster with New Departure brakes, the finest, and a front-end shock absorber that stuck out from the front forks. "Too bad," Sheehan said. "I guess you're too little."

"You can't ride much out in the country," I pointed out.

His lip curled. "Do you even know how to ride?"

"What do you guys want, anyway?"

"Where's the mutt?"

"At the side of the house. Why?"

"You got to see this," Sheehan told Inright. "Come on."

They walked to the corner of the house. I followed nervously. Skipper got up from the shade and growled.

"It's okay, Skipper," I said.

"You see?" Sheehan said. "Dumb mutt is looking in the wrong direction. Can't see a thing."

"I never saw anything like it!" Inright said.

Sheehan picked up a pebble and chunked it at Skipper. It hit his side and he yelped. Sheehan laughed.

"Stop that!" I said.

He picked up another rock. "Are you gonna make me?"

From the back of the house came my mother. She smiled at the others. "Hello there! Are you friends of Danny's?—Why, you're the Sheehan boy. You were here with your parents, right?"

"That's right," Sheehan said. "Howdy do, ma'am?" He was suddenly all smiles and charm. "This is Phil Inright. We came by to tell Danny hello."

"Well, isn't that nice! I have some iced tea inside if you would like some. You look all hot from riding those bikes all the way out here."

"That sure sounds nice," Sheehan told her, "but we got to go. Thank you a lot."

"Well, come back when you have more time, you hear?"

"Yes, ma'am." He nudged Inright. "Come on."

Leaving her there with Skipper, the three of us walked back to the front driveway.

"We'll be back, Flatfoot," Sheehan said.

"Good riddance to bad rubbish," I told him.

"I won't get even today for the way you hit me when my back was turned that day at school, but I ain't forgot it."

Thunder rolled overhead. It had rapidly clouded up again. I did not say anything. I had thought I was safe for the summer. But their bikes, I saw, gave them just enough mobility to come out here at any time. It was a dismaying realization.

"So long, Danny," Inright said. He was not a bad kid, but totally under Sheehan's domination. By himself, I thought, he might even be a friend. But with Sheehan he had to be the enemy. I think he would have tried to kill me—without rancor and with a sense of regret—if Sheehan had ordered it.

"Ride carefully," I told him.

They swung onto their bikes and pedaled out onto the highway. Both of them stood on the pedals, pumping hard into the freshening north breeze, and within moments they were out of view to the north, back toward Harmony. I went back to Skipper and petted him to make up for the rock. New thunder came, and a flash of lightning in the clouds. The rain started again. Skipper and I ran for the house.

12

For two more days it rained almost continuously. Behind the house, the creek came out of its banks again. The garden lay flattened, a slick of black mud, with even the cornstalks beaten to a severe angle.

"If it doesn't break soon," my father said at the supper table, "we're going to have some serious flooding. They're getting ready for it in town. They've got thousands of empty sandbags that have been delivered to the gym, and they're talking about evacuating everybody on the flats."

"If the creek out back gets much higher," my mother said, "I'm going to start worrying about *our* evacuating."

"Oh, I don't think it will affect us in that way. You can already see where it's starting to spill over into the fields on the Dawkins place. We're on good, high ground. In Harmony . . . that's a different matter."

"It worries me anyway."

"I know. The first time we get a break, I'm going to get a crew back out here and do it right this time. We'll deepen the channel and take out that bend. On downstream a mile or so there's another area that impedes the current. We'll clean that out, too."

"Why don't they work on the Big Walnut," I asked, "to make it stop flooding the same way?"

"Well, they are, bit by bit. But that's a mighty big project. It's going to take years."

"What do they do if it just keeps raining?"

"It's a very serious thing, son. Harmony was originally founded in a curve of the river, and that was fine when it was a source of water that could easily be tapped and Harmony consisted of a couple dozen families. But now the town has grown so that the business section is just below that curve. They tell me that during the big flood in the thirties, the river just took a short cut, eliminating the bend. If it tries to do that ever again, it will cover most of downtown."

"A few sandbags won't help that much!"

"The plan is to pile the sandbags on the banks all along the curve. Hold it back there, and the worst they'll have is some minor flooding down around the park."

"That sounds like a lot of sandbags, boy!"

"It is a lot of sandbags."

He said the normal level of the river through Harmony was fourteen feet, and that at the present time it stood at seventeen. The serious flooding of 1932 or 1933 had started when the river reached the nineteen-foot level and spilled over its banks. Channel work since that time had put the spill point at twenty feet precisely. Several leaders of the town had already been to the statehouse in Columbus, trying to get help in case the rain kept coming. The governor had pledged some National Guard trucks and as many state police as he could spare. But already they were flooded north and east of Columbus, and around Dayton. Ohio River towns were beginning to prepare for that mighty waterway to rise dangerously. The more my father talked, the more serious things sounded. I could tell he and my mother were troubled.

The rain continued through the night, but slacked to drizzle by morning. The creek behind the house had tumbled chunks of trees and trash all over the lower slope, and water gleamed in the fields beyond. The rushing brown torrent made ugly foam along its edges, tugging away chunks of the earth in little avalanches. My father left for work a little before eight, and was back before ten. "We're going to have a shot at clearing some of that out right away before the rain picks up again," he said.

It was exciting when the truck of prisoners pulled into the driveway. The rain had stopped, although the sky was swollen. Watching in the front window, Aggie jumped up and down.

"Look, Mommy, look! There are lots of them!"

About a dozen prisoners climbed out with their shovels. In addition to the driver there were three other guards. I was atuned to the fact that work details evidently worked by areas, so my friend Rudi should be on this job. I did not see him at first, but then I spied him in the back of the group as they trooped around the house. In the bedroom, Skipper heard them and started going crazy.

My father, who had gone outside to speak to the guards, came back in momentarily. "Squirt, tie Skipper outside awhile. It looks like it's going to clear temporarily and he can bark his head off out there without breaking everybody's eardrums."

By the time I got Skipper out and tied to his stake, the work detail had gone down the slope and farther upstream. From the house I could not see them at all. My father came around the house, wearing rubber boots and a raincoat that swirled in the freshening breeze. "Want to go with me, Squirt?"

"Yeah!"

"Get your boots on. Hurry."

I rushed to the back porch and buckled on my galoshes. When I rejoined my father and we started away, Skipper started whining.

"Not this time, Skipper. All we need is for you to fall in."

We mushed past the garden, through the beaten-down brush, and into the little orchard that sloped toward the creek. The roar of its water came to us before we could see it from this direction. When we did get it in view, I was numbed by how broad it had become here, foaming with its power where it boiled around a bend. The prisoners were already at work freeing debris that had piled up to form a partial dam across the channel. Others, with big saws, were starting to cut down several willows that the rushing water had undermined.

It was hard, muddy, dangerous work. My father and I watched for some time. Overhead, the thick clouds parted a bit and a few stray shafts of sunlight came through. It seemed a good omen. The smaller willows were cut and dragged well back from the creek so they could not fall and start a new damming action. The timber dam that had formed in the last few days was broken loose, pieces surging down with the current. The level along the curve appeared to drop a bit, leaving gleaming mud banks high and dry.

I watched Rudi doing his part. He had helped saw some of the trees, and he now had a shovel, was using it to pry pieces of debris out of the mud near the bank and carry them well back. He was muddy and he looked tired, and his limp was more noticeable. I felt sorry for him.

"Dad, don't you think it's time they got a rest?"

"The head guard decides that, son."

I looked the guards over. Three were civilians, older men standing aside with their rifles at ease, merely watching. The fourth was an army man, sergeant's stripes sewed on the sleeves of his fatigues. The cap pulled well down on his forehead served to make him look tougher. He had slab features, vigilant eyes. His carbine was slung over his shoulder, but he missed nothing. He moved from place to place, his putteed boots heavy in the muck, giving an instruction here and pointing something out there. When he gestured at Rudi, clearly telling him to work faster, I knew I did not like him.

The work at the curve was almost finished. The crew moved farther along the bank, nearer the house, clearing more debris. There were some larger breaks in the clouds now and the sun gleamed on water everywhere. The creek smelled rank, of green vegetation and the mud. My father and I walked along with the crew, staying back out of the way.

"Well," my father said, "maybe the weatherman is wrong again." He shaded his face with his hand as he eyed the clouds. "They say more tonight. I certainly hope he's wrong."

I sat on a soggy stump. "I'm getting tired. I bet these guys would like a rest by *now*."

My father looked at me a moment, then signaled the sergeant, who strode over to us. He was a grim, unsmiling man, all business.

"Yes, sir?"

"Sergeant, isn't it about time for a break?"

"Sir, there's a lot to be done along here." The man's eyes were bleak, giving nothing.

My father's jaw set. "Give them ten minutes' rest, Sergeant."

"Yes, sir." The sergeant turned and reached for his whistle. It shrilled. "Ten minutes!" he barked. He walked to a nearby tree and stood beside it, hands clasped rigidly behind his back in parade rest. He was angry about the break.

I watched the men find stumps or fallen trees to use for seats. Putting their tools down, they sank down thankfully. Rudi, one of those nearest the water, squatted where he was and took a pack of cigarettes—*my* pack—from his pocket. He lit one, looked toward us, and raised his hand in a light salute. I waved to him and signaled him to join us. He smiled and shook his head.

"Who are you waving at?" my father asked.

"Rudi. Over there."

"One of the prisoners?"

"Yes. He's my friend."

"Your *friend?*"

"He's always in the gang that works in this area. He noticed Skipper. He knows everything about dogs and stuff. He had a blind dog when he was a kid. He made me a leash for Skipper and told me lots of stuff to help train him."

My father's frown was puzzled. "A *prisoner?*"

"Sure!"

"Well I'll be damned," he said softly. "Which one is he?"

"Over there." I waved. "Hey, Rudi!" Rudi nodded in response.

My father started toward him, picking his way among the others. I followed closely. As we neared Rudi, he got nervously to his feet and came to a semblance of attention. His stiff carriage reminded me sharply of the German warrior he had been.

"I understand you and my son are friends," my father said.

Rudi smiled. "Yes, sir. It is so. You have a very fine boy."

My father was watching him with quiet intensity. "You gave him some pointers about the dog?"

"Yes, sir. I am—I was a veterinarian. In Munich. I had a dog like this of my own before the war."

"What barracks are you in, Rudi?"

"Six, sir."

"And you had a blind dog?"

"One much like Danny's, sir. *Ja.*"

My father looked at me. "No wonder you knew all those tricks to get his attention and teach him to obey. I never thought you were going to be able to do it. But you did. Now I begin to see how."

"It was easy, with Rudi giving me tips," I said.

Rudi shook his head. "It cannot be easy, sir. Most such animals must be put away. Everything must be done for such a pet. Everything. Your son has put in many more hours than you can imagine."

"I know he's worked hard."

"To do as he has done requires a heroic effort, sir. Nothing less."

My father looked at Rudi for what seemed a long time. Then he turned to me. He appeared at a loss. "And you two worked on it together."

"He did it all, sir," Rudi said. "We see each other only a few minutes at a time, during a rest like this. I gave suggestions only."

"He knows everything, though," I pointed out.

"Are you being treated all right, Rudi?"

"Yes, sir. Fine."

My father glanced at the sergeant, who had begun pacing back and forth. "It looks like time to get back to work. Maybe we can talk more later, Rudi."

"It would be my pleasure, sir."

My father led me back across the work site. The sergeant's whistle shrilled. Work resumed.

"He's a great guy, isn't he, Dad?" I asked.

"You're not bad yourself," he replied.

When lunch time rolled around, the work was far from finished. We hiked back to the house while the prisoners and guards ate out of their metal boxes. The weather had continued to improve, and my mother needed to go into town for groceries. As my father intended to remain here until the work was done, it was agreed that my mother would take Aggie in the car and drive to Harmony. We had eggs and biscuits for lunch.

After Mother and Aggie departed, my father finished his cigarette and went to the barn for the ladder. Putting it on the side of the house, he climbed onto the roof with hammer and nails and tar paper, and tacked down several layers over a spot which he thought had been the source of a slight leak in all the rain. He then walked around the sloping composition roof, examining it. Finally he climbed down. He said there were some other spots that looked suspicious, but he could not fix them alone.

"I'll help," I said.

"You on that roof? Not on your life."

"Rudi will help you, then," I suggested eagerly.

"Well, that might not be a bad idea. He can hold the paper while I nail, and then pay a visit to Skipper. What do you think?"

"Great! He's never seen how we do the game with the ball."

Skipper pulled at his rope, whining again, as we headed off. I told him to be patient and we would be right back. We went down the hill through the mud, the hot sunlight making it seem like steam was rising around us.

"How did you meet Rudi, Squirt?"

"They were working over there in the other field, and they needed water, and they came over here, and he saw me with Skipper and saw he was blind."

"When Skipper was little?"

"Right after we got him."

"What do you and Rudi talk about besides Skipper?"

"Oh, we talked about the war, some. He was in Africa."

"What does he say about the war?"

"He says he'll be glad when it's over and he can go home."

"Does he talk about Hitler?"

"Not really. Why?"

"I was just wondering. Come on. I'll help you climb over, here."

We reached the area where the work of clearing the banks continued. My father walked over to the sergeant and spoke to him, pointing up toward the higher ground where the house was hidden by the trees and terrain. The sergeant frowned and nodded agreement, then turned and signaled one of the civilian guards. The two men conferred. The civilian then walked across the site to where Rudi was sawing a branch. They spoke, and Rudi started toward us, the guard at his side.

"Rudi doesn't need a darn *guard,*" I told my father.

"Humor the sergeant," my father said. "Besides, he can hold the ladder for us."

Rudi reached us. "You need some help at your house, sir?"

"Some roofing has blown loose. I can't hold it in place and nail a new piece down at the same time. Can you give me a hand?"

"Of course," Rudi said. "It is permitted to smoke while we walk up the hill?"

My father took out a Chesterfield and gave Rudi one. Then, cupping his hands around the match, he lit both cigarettes. We started up the hill with the guard trailing us.

"Wait till you see the game with the ball, Rudi!" I told him. "Old Skipper catches that ball before it bounces twice!"

"Then does he bring it back to you?"

"Sometimes he does. Sometimes he just lays down with it and makes me take it from him."

Rudi chuckled. "I think the dog believes he has taught *you* a game."

"I'm going to go get the ball and show you!" I ran ahead through the brush, allowing them to walk along at their slower pace. I was deliriously happy. My father and Rudi had met, and my father had given him a cigarette. That showed how much he liked Rudi. Now that they had met, maybe there would be other odd jobs around the house, and Rudi would come more often. Everything was going to be better now.

I ran up past the muddy garden, heading for the house. Sunlight played around my feet as I went. I thought I knew exactly where the hollow ball was. I remembered leaving it in the pantry.

Just as I passed the garden, however, I heard a sharp yelp of pain ahead—from Skipper. From this angle I could not see where I had left him tied. Hurrying faster, I thought the cats were tormenting him. But hadn't they been left in the house?

I heard Skipper yelp again, then whine.

I rounded the corner of the house.

The first thing I saw was the two bicycles—the red Fleetwing and the battered blue Roadmaster—parked in the driveway. Then I saw Skipper, turning around and around on himself at the end of his rope. He was still whining, baffled and hurt. Then I saw Sheehan and Inright nearer the house, out of Skipper's reach. Sheehan had a handful of small rocks held with his left hand against his chest. As I watched, he took another rock and, with his right hand, hurled it at Skipper. It hit Skipper in the hindquarters and he danced in pain, yelping again. Sheehan was laughing.

"Stop that!" I yelled.

They both saw me. Inright took a step backward nearer the bikes. Sheehan held his ground, tossing another rock lightly in his hand.

I ran to Skipper. He was turning around and around in confusion. I threw myself down beside him, hugging his neck. "It's okay, Skipper! It's okay now, boy! They won't do it anymore!" I buried my face in his thick fur. "You're safe now, boy!" He twisted around gladly, with intense relief, licking frantically at my face.

A rock stung my back.

I scrambled to my feet. Turning, I faced Sheehan and Inright. Sheehan must have seen something in my eyes because he dropped the rest of his rocks and started to turn away. Inright had already started toward the bikes and now Sheehan broke into a run after him.

I was unhinged. What they had done to me was one thing. But they had tormented Skipper, whose blindness and rope made him helpless. I was filled with a crazy rage, and my legs had never carried me faster as I chased them. As I closed the distance, I saw Inright get on his bike and start to pump away. Sheehan got a leg up, but was off balance and staggered.

I crashed into him, knocking both him and the bicycle over. The impact jarred me, but I hardly noticed. I was punching blindly—as blindly as my Skipper—and some of the blows were landing. I hit him in the eye and the nose and we rolled over, fighting back. Behind us, Skipper was going crazy, barking as I had never heard him bark before.

Sheehan managed to stick his fingers in my eye. I yelled and fell back, and he was instantly on top of me. He hit me hard, but in the effort lost his balance and fell to the side. I kicked him and rolled over on top of him again, swinging hysterically.

"You won't *ever* pick on a dog again," I panted, hitting him on the ear. "You think you're so *tough*"—the chin—"but you're just a big *bully*"—the nose—"and I'm gonna show *you*"—the nose again.

"I give!" Sheehan cried, trying to cover up, kicking. I was aware of adults rushing up toward us, but I kept hitting him. "I give, Flatfoot! Ow! Ouch! Stop! Ow! I *give!*"

I stopped hitting him. Sitting astride his chest, I held my fist ready. "You promise?"

He kicked me off, hit me on the side of the head, and piled on top of me, pummeling me with both hands.

Someone—Rudi—had reached us. He tried to separate us. We were both writhing dervishes, punching wildly. Rudi anxiously grabbed Sheehan's arm and pulled him away. Sheehan swung around awkwardly and something made a popping noise in his shoulder.

"*Ow!*" Sheehan screamed, going limp in Rudi's grasp. "You killed me! You broke my arm! Help! Help! He's killing me!"

The guard rushed up behind Rudi. I saw his expression and how completely he had misunderstood. He had the rifle raised in a lethal position.

"*No!*" I cried. "He's—"

Too late. The butt of the rifle crashed into Rudi's skull with a sickening sound and he went down like a feed sack.

Horrified, I stared. The guard looked down at Rudi, then at Sheehan, who was writhing around like he had been tortured. My father ran up. The guard bent over Rudi as if he was going to hit him again.

I attacked the guard. I was screaming words, but had no idea what they were. I beat at him with my fists in such fury that he actually was staggered backward. I felt him trying to dislodge me. Then my father was there, grappling with me, lifting me bodily into the air.

"Calm down!" he ordered. "Calm down!"

"You've killed him!" I shrilled. "You've killed my Rudi! I'll get you for it if it's the last thing I ever do!"

13

We used the camp truck to hurry Rudi to the small clinic in Harmony. My father and I rode in the back with him, and his blanket-wrapped form did not move during the hard, jouncing trip. I think I was on the edge of hysteria. My father kept his arm around me.

"He's going to be all right, Squirt," he told me. "You see? He isn't bleeding. It doesn't feel like his skull was fractured."

"I hate this place!" I retorted. "I hate the town and the school and that guard and the colonel and *everybody!* And I'm going to get even!"

"I know, Squirt. I know. But he's going to be all right."

Bill Sheehan and Phil Inright were in the front with the guard, who was driving. When I last saw him, Sheehan had still been writhing in pain. Someone had said something about shoulder dislocation. "I hope it's been torn out by the roots!" I had screamed.

When we reached the clinic, my father hurried inside. Moments later, I peered out and saw the sergeant helping Sheehan, who was weeping and grimacing, through the heavy glass doors

of the entryway. Then the doors swung again and two people—
my father and a heavyset nurse—rushed out with a stretcher on
a dolly of some kind. A man in shirtsleeves, probably a doctor,
followed. The three of them managed to get Rudi onto the
stretcher and down to ground level. The doctor and nurse
wheeled him inside. My father lifted me down and we followed.

In the lobby of the building, a dozen or more patients, older
people, sat on the periphery. Back beyond the reception desk,
which was vacant, was a hallway to treatment rooms. I heard
Sheehan hollering. Phil Inright sat on a chair next to the hallway. He looked scared to death.

My father took me over to chairs beside him. "Are you all
right?" he asked Inright.

"Yessir, I guess," Phil said huskily.

My father looked around grimly. "I've got to make some
calls." He dug into his pocket. "You boys want a Coke or
something?"

"No!" I said. How could he think about Cokes at a time like
this?

He went to a pay phone booth on the far side of the lobby.
Inright cracked his knuckles. "Boy. Bill is hurt bad."

"I hope the queerbait dies," I snapped.

"He's going to be in a lot of trouble if you tell about him
chunking rocks at your dog, Danny."

"What do you think I'm going to do? Say Skipper was
chunking them at *him?*"

"His dad is real mean to him sometimes. Maybe we could
just say—"

"Listen, Phil," I hissed, squeezing his arm as hard as I could.
"If you lie to protect Sheehan, I'll get you if it's the last thing I
ever do!"

Inright stared at me. He looked paler.

"I mean it," I told him. "I'll beat you up every day of your
life after school. I'll—I'll go find Benny Harrison and have *him*
get you!"

"I'll tell the truth! I'll tell the truth!"

"I'm going to be watching you. You better!"

We sat miserably for a few minutes. My father was making

calls. Sheehan had stopped yelling. *What was happening to Rudi?*

"We didn't mean any harm," Inright told me miserably. "We just come out to see you."

"That's a lie right there. Sheehan came out to beat up on me if he could. And he dragged you along like a big piece of stupid blubber to stand and watch."

"Your dog started growling when we rode up."

"So you had to chunk rocks at him?"

"I didn't chunk any rocks!"

"You let Sheehan!"

"I didn't think it would hurt your dumb old dog!"

I almost hit him right then and there. "Just remember what I told you. If you don't tell the truth—*all* the truth—you'll wish you was dead when I get you later!"

"I will! I will!"

My father came back. He gave Inright a stony glance. "Your parents are on the way. I also talked to Mr. Sheehan and Colonel Thatcher."

"My mom and dad know?" Inright groaned.

My father sat down beside me. "Now all we can do is wait."

I sat in agony, swinging my legs. Outside came a roll of thunder, signifying that the weatherman had not been wrong after all. The receptionist came back out to the desk. The older folks in the room waited, covertly watching us or looking at ancient copies of the *Saturday Evening Post*.

In a few minutes the man in shirtsleeves came out and walked over. My father stood to greet him with the expression of a man bracing himself.

"The boy has a dislocation and possible muscle damage," the doctor said. "He'll be all right, but we want more X rays. The German appears to have a slight concussion, but he's conscious now and sitting up."

"Rudi's okay?" I said with intense relief.

The doctor ignored me. "What we want to do is send both of them to Columbus. I think the boy will probably need a shoulder cast, but he ought to be ambulatory in an hour or two. The German ought to be observed overnight, just as a precaution."

"Is there an ambulance?"

"We've sent for one."

The front doors swung open. Mr. and Mrs. Sheehan boiled in. Mrs. Sheehan was wearing a housecoat and her hair was in curlers. She was crying. "My baby!" she wept. "Where is my baby boy?"

"He's all right, Mrs. Sheehan," the doctor assured her.

"I want to see him! Where is he?"

"He's in the treatment room, Mrs. Sheehan, and—"

"What happened?" Sheehan demanded angrily. "By God! A boy goes riding on his bicycle and gets attacked in broad daylight by some Nazi fanatic? I—"

"It was hardly that way," my father cut in. "The prisoner was trying to separate your boy and mine. They were fighting."

"Fighting!" Sheehan's bulging eyes rolled to me. "Were you picking on Bill again? You ought to be disciplined severely. George, this is not the first time there's been trouble between these boys. I hope *now*—when something this serious has happened—you'll take some effective action!"

"I never picked on him!" I said. "He picked on *me!*"

"Only a few days ago, boy, my son came home all muddy, where you had attacked him without provocation—"

"That's a lie!"

Mrs. Sheehan wailed, "I want to see my baby!"

"This way," the doctor said, and they followed him down the hall.

My father looked down at me.

"It's a lie!" I repeated, frantic.

"Did you knock the Sheehan boy down at school?"

"Yes! But—"

"I don't know where this is going to end," he cut in. "First you're thick as hops with that delinquent. Then this. What's *happened* to you? You were always a good boy . . . a gentle boy. Since we moved to Harmony, you've been nothing but trouble."

It was the worst possible time to lose my composure, but my universe was crumbling. I could not help it. The tears rolled. "*Dad!* It's not that way at all! *He* was the one! He—"

The front door swung open again and a burly man wearing a butcher's apron came in, thick arms swinging. He saw us and churned over, eyes on Inright. "What's happened?" he demanded.

"Pop," Inright gasped, "Bill Sheehan got hurt, but he's going to be okay! I'm fine!" He looked scared to death.

"What happened?" the man repeated. He glared at my father.

"I'm George Davidson. You must be Mr. Inright." He held out his hand.

The man ignored it. "I know who you are. You're the one coddling those Nazis out there. What have *you* got to do with this?"

"The Sheehan boy was hurt at our place." My father's face was flushed.

Inright's father wheeled on him. "What were you doing out there? Have I told you? Have I *told* you?" His fists balled. I thought he was going to hit Phil.

"We was just riding our bikes!" Phil choked.

"Riding your bikes out there? Listen, boy, you'd better talk fast!"

Phil looked dreadful, eyes wide, face the color of bread dough. Saliva dribbled down his chin. "We went for a ride. We"—he glanced fearfully at me—"we stopped at Danny's house. Nobody was around—"

"Then what happened?" his father demanded loudly.

Phil hesitated. He was torn between fears. I watched him, agonized.

"What *happened?*" his father repeated, shaking him roughly.

"Then *he* came up," Phil said, pointing at me. "And he started punching Bill—and hitting him—and I wasn't doing nothing, just standing there—and this German ran up, and he pulled Bill away from the fight, only he hurt him."

"A *German* hurt the Sheehan boy?"

"Yeah! He—"

"Davidson, what was a German doing where he could attack innocent kids?"

"It's not quite the way your boy told it," my father said. "We—"

"Don't call my son a liar!"

"I'm not. He's just excited. I saw the last part of what happened. My son and the Sheehan boy were fighting. The prisoner tried to pull them apart—"

"What was a German *doing* there?"

"There was a work detail."

The man was shaking with anger. He was big, powerful, menacing, very nearly out of control. He turned back to Phil. "Where's your bike?"

"Out at Danny's house. We—"

"We'll go get it. Right now. Then we'll have the rest of this out." He grabbed Phil's neck roughly in his big hand and started to turn him away from us.

"Wait!" I said. "He hasn't told all of it!"

Mr. Inright wheeled back. "What's that?"

I backed up a step, cowering involuntarily. "He hasn't told all of it yet." I looked at Phil imploringly. "Phil. Tell him the rest of it. *Please.*"

Phil hesitated. He was trembling. His father still had him clamped in a harsh grip by the neck as if he were a possession.

"Is there more?" his father growled.

"They was fighting," Phil said hoarsely. "And the German—"

His father shook him so his teeth rattled. *"Is there more? Do you know what happens when you lie to me?"*

"Yes, sir! Yes, sir!" Phil's eyes rolled back. "There wasn't any more—that's all of it—I didn't do nothing bad!"

Inright started for the door. "I'll talk to you later!" he flung back at my father.

My father looked down at me. I had never seen him so grim and angry.

"I didn't beat up on Bill Sheehan," I said. "He beat up on *me*. All I did, finally, was hit back, the way Benny taught me. And—"

"Benny Harrison again? Sit down there and be quiet!" There was a tone in his voice I had never heard before. It was contempt.

Somehow we found my mother in town. There was a silent, shaken ride back to the house. The bicycles were gone and so was the work crew. Drizzle came down steadily. My father said he had to go to Columbus to see how Rudi and Bill Sheehan were. When he started off the porch, I did not ask if I could go; I simply followed him. He gave me an angry look as I climbed into the front seat beside him, but he let me come.

The ride to Columbus was made in frigid silence. Rain pelted the car.

The hospital was a great, gloomy red brick building on the city's south side. We parked and hurried through the rain. I sat on a wooden bench while my father made inquiries. Gray-faced, he turned and signaled for me to join him. Then we walked down a long, glistening corridor with tall wooden doors on either side looking into rooms with white beds and people lying in them.

At the corner we turned right. Passing a nursing station, we proceeded. Up ahead I saw a soldier standing beside a closed door. He had a rifle. The colonel was pacing up and down, boots clicking on the tile. When he saw us, he hurried to intercept us.

"This is terrible, Davidson," he said tightly. "This is the worst."

"How are they?" my father asked.

"The Sheehan boy was put in a shoulder cast and sent home. Looked like he was still in a lot of pain. Our prisoner is in there. They say they'll release him tomorrow morning."

My relief was intense. "Can I talk to him?"

"Boy," the colonel snapped, "it appears to me you've done enough damage for one day!"

"Leave him alone," my father said. "I've already talked to him about it."

"Talked? Is that all you're going to do?"

"He's *my* boy, Colonel. Stay out of it."

Colonel Thatcher's cheeks were ruddy. "We've had a prisoner attack an innocent child, Davidson. The parents are beside themselves, and I can't say I blame them. My telephone was ringing off the wall when I left. The community is riled up. This is going to make things even more difficult for us."

"All Rudi did was pull the boys apart. It was an accident with Sheehan."

"By Gadfrey I don't care *what* you want to call it! This is the last straw! What were you doing with a work crew on your personal property anyway?"

"They were clearing the drainage ditch. You signed that work order yesterday."

"This child-butcher in this room didn't attack that boy at the ditch. He did it in your front yard!"

"He was stopping a fight!"

"What was he doing in your front yard?"

"He was going to help me fix a leak in my roof."

"Work on personal property? That's a clear violation of regulations, Davidson. A *clear* violation of regulations."

My father's jaw set. He was angrier than I had ever seen him. He didn't say a word.

The colonel said, "We'll transport the prisoner to the camp in the morning. He'll be interviewed and put in the stockade until further notice. When this has been straightened out, there will be a hearing about your participation in all this. I understand there is a meeting starting in Harmony at this very hour. I must get there at once."

"You've got it all wrong!" I protested.

The colonel did not so much as look at me. He turned and strode down the hall toward the exit.

I stared at my father. He stood stiff. The angry color had gone from his face. He was looking straight ahead in shock.

"It's not like they all said," I told him.

He looked at me. "What?"

"It wasn't the way they said," I repeated.

"Danny, don't you think we've had quite enough from you today?"

"Ask Rudi. Just ask Rudi, Dad!"

He thought about it, then squared his shoulders with resignation. He turned to the soldier blocking the hospital room door. "We want to go in for a minute, Private."

The soldier stood stiffly. "Sir! My orders are to admit only necessary medical personnel."

"Private, do you know who I am?"

"Sir! You are the civilian overseer for all guard personnel, sir!"

"Then I think you'd better get out of our way, Private, don't you?"

The young soldier looked at my father for a moment. My father waited unblinkingly. I could see the wheels turning in the soldier's head. After another few seconds he stepped smartly to the side. "Sir!" he said.

The room was dimly lighted. In the lone bed, Rudi lay in a sea of white sheets. There was a thick gauze bandage around his head. He was almost as pale as the bedding, but he turned his head to watch us as we approached.

"Are you all right, Rudi?" I whispered.

He nodded, smiling faintly. "Dizzy only. Fine."

"That guard was a dopus," I told him. "He was a queerbait. I'll get even with him—"

"All right, Squirt," my father said. "That's enough."

"I—"

"I said, that's enough!"

I bit my tongue.

Rudi looked at my father. "The other boy?"

"His shoulder was hurt. Some kind of dislocation. He's gone home now. In a cast."

Rudi's face twisted. "Ach."

"There will probably be charges."

"Because I hurt the boy. Yes. I see."

"Possibly against both of us."

Rudi looked surprised. "You?"

"The colonel says I broke regulations, bringing you to the house."

Rudi's smile was bitter. "Yes. Regulations. Colonels are the same in all armies, it seems."

"Rudi, what were they fighting about? Did you see?"

"No. When I turned the corner, they were already fighting. I was afraid one would get hurt. The other boy had a rock in his hand."

"The Sheehan boy had a rock?"

"*Ja.* He—"

"He was hitting Skipper with rocks," I said. "That's what I've been trying to tell you!"

"Wait a minute. Let me get this straight. The Sheehan and Inright boys were throwing rocks at your dog?"

"Sheehan was. Phil's so dumb, he was just standing there."

"I didn't hear the Inright boy tell his father that."

"He was afraid his dad would kill him, probably."

My father's forehead was a washboard. "So you ran up and saw the Sheehan boy hitting Skipper with rocks."

"He was standing back where Skipper couldn't get at him, 'cause of the rope, and he was chunking rocks, hitting Skipper. And Skipper was crying, and he didn't know what was going on because he's blind and all, and I just—Sheehan calls me Flatfoot, Dad, and he always *picks* on me, that's why I got Benny to teach me how to fight, and when I saw him hitting Skipper with rocks, I just lit into him."

"And then Rudi came up and tried to separate you," my father said quietly, a different expression on his face.

"That's the truth, Dad! I swear it!"

He put his hands on his hips. "Well. It explains a lot of things. I'll look into it." He sighed. "I don't know how much good I'll do. If those other boys lie, their parents will believe them, not you or me. And I can just imagine the way this is all going over in Harmony. 'An innocent boy attacked by one of our prisoners.' That's what they're saying right now."

"You can make 'em see the truth, Dad!"

"I don't know, Squirt." He gave Rudi a determined glance. "You can be sure I'll try."

My relief was so deep it was almost painful. I looked at Rudi. He winked at me. I reached out for his hand and he gave it. On impulse I leaned over the high edge of the bed and kissed him. His cheek was rough with stubble.

"Such a boy!" he said softly. "Such a boy!"

My father put his arm around me. I let go and bawled like a baby.

14

The rain came down steadily all night, and when my father left for the camp early in the morning, water was standing in our front yard and we could see the creek behind the house, its water creeping dangerously close to the back end of the ruined garden. We had pans under three leaks that had now developed in the roof. I put on my slicker and took Skipper out briefly, leading him back through and into my room where he shook himself vigorously, spraying everything in sight. I cleaned that up and went back to the living room, where my mother had started ironing. The Zenith was playing on the table.

"And now the news at eight," the announcer said. *"On the local scene, new downpours have put several creeks and rivers out of their banks in central and south-central Ohio. About two hundred residents were evacuated during the night in Chillicothe. In West Jefferson, power has been off since midnight. Officials warn that forecasts of more rain—up to another six inches in some areas—will mean heavy local flooding.*

"Worst hit so far are the communities of Groveport and Reynoldsburg. However, officials warn that the Big Walnut is

rising fast and could threaten Harmony and other towns in the south within thirty to forty-eight hours."

"Mom! He said—"

"Hush, Danny! Listen."

"In Harmony, Mayor E. L. Gump has ordered emergency action along the notorious Harmony curve in the Big Walnut. City and county crews have already begun filling and placing sandbags. An emergency meeting of the town has been called for four o'clock today.

"In other news at this hour—"

"It's going to flood!" I said excitedly.

"Maybe not," my mother said. But she looked worried.

Skipper came nosing out of my room. He walked slowly, unerringly, to the hall doorway, turned, and came in. He padded slowly, tail wagging. He veered slightly to avoid my father's chair, then started toward his favorite living room spot under the west window. My mother and the ironing board were in his way.

"You'll have to go around, Skipper," my mother said, ironing.

He stopped at the sound of her voice and waited, tongue lolling. His tail wagged.

"Skipper," I said. "Here."

He turned to his left a bit and walked toward the sound of my voice. I grasped his collar and led him around the ironing board and to the window area. He turned around once, sniffing to orient himself, and then lay down.

"I suppose I'll never be able to rearrange the furniture," my mother sighed.

"He can relearn it," I told her.

"Is he all right? Those stones the boy threw didn't hurt him?"

"I can't see anything. He kind of jerks when I press a couple of places, though."

"Your father told me everything that happened. I only hope your prisoner friend isn't in too much trouble."

"I hope *Rudi* isn't in too much trouble."

"You like Rudi very much, don't you?"

"He's a great guy, Mom. I don't think I could have *ever* trained Skipper if it hadn't been for him."

She looked surprised. "I can't imagine you've seen all that much of him."

"It's not that I've seen him a lot. Gosh, that's impossible, him being a prisoner, and all. But when he did see me, he was real interested. He told me exactly what to do. You know how Skipper walks beside me? He told me about that, and how to teach him. He—"

"How about the way you feed Skipper cookies behind my back? Did your Rudi teach you that, too?"

"I thought of that myself," I admitted sheepishly.

"I just thought you did!"

"But Rudi said you have to reward a dog when he does good. And since your cookies are the greatest thing in the world, I thought—"

"Danny," she said archly. "You're talking like a Philadelphia lawyer to me again."

"Aw, Mom!"

Aggie came out of the bedroom hall, dragging her favorite small flannel blanket and sucking her fingers. The cats, Christopher and Mewbox, gamboled out with her, ran across the room, and attacked Skipper's ears. His tail thumped. He closed his eyes and shook his head lazily, trying to make them stop.

It rained steadily all morning. At noon my father drove in through a steady drizzle and ate his lunch on the kitchen table. He was worried and grim.

"The Big Walnut is over eighteen feet," he told us. "They've started to sandbag on both sides around the curve. The governor is sending a few state police and national guardsmen—reserves—but he can't spare many because a lot of towns are facing the same thing. They're asking for all volunteers. There's going to be a general meeting at the fire station at three o'clock. I think I'd better be there. Chances are, I'll stay and work."

"Are the prisoners going to be used?" my mother asked.

"The colonel volunteered them. The city fathers"—his voice was ironic—"refused."

"That's ridiculous."

He glanced at me. "Yesterday capped things off. I understand some of the stories are pretty wild. By the time it gets through another few retellings, we'll have had a mass breakout with pillage and mayhem all over the place."

"Is Rudi all right?" I asked.

"Rudi is in a detention cell at the camp. I saw him. He's fine."

"It's not fair, putting him in a cell!"

"We'll try to get that sorted out later, Squirt. Right now, the flood takes precedence."

"George," my mother said, "I think all of us ought to come into Harmony with you this afternoon."

"Why?" He was surprised.

"Go look at our creek."

He got up and went out into the kitchen. When he came back he was grimmer. "I don't think it will go much higher, but you're right. No sense anyone being stuck out here . . . getting their toes wet."

"Can the kitties go?" Aggie piped up.

"Yes, the kitties can go."

"And Skipper?" I chimed in.

He sighed. "And Skipper, yes."

The rain drummed down hard while we prepared in a carnival atmosphere. Aggie ran in and out of her room at least twenty times, asking if she could take such-and-so. The cats caught the excitement and were everywhere but on the ceiling. My father dressed in heavy work clothing and boots, with a long slicker and cap. My mother made a few sandwiches for the picnic basket. By the time she went around needlessly checking windows and doors, it was well past two o'clock. We set out in a steady drizzle.

Along the way we saw a lot of flooding. Broad fields lay like gray lakes. When we crossed the Big Walnut south of Harmony, the muddy water was within two feet of the pavement, boiling with ugly foam. We could feel the structure trembling as we drove over it. Farther along, a little creek had come over the highway and we drove slowly, water sloshing under the fenders and running boards, until we reached higher ground again and everyone breathed easier. The drizzle continued to slacken, and when we drove down Main Street it was little more than a mist. Cars and trucks had their headlights on, however, because the clouds overhead were so low they appeared in reach. Lightning veined them periodically, and the rumble of thunder was constant.

Townspeople were flocking toward the fire station from all directions. We had to park a block away. The old Ford fire truck had been parked out on the wet concrete apron, the garage to be used for the meeting. Officials had packed chairs wall to wall, but these were already all occupied when we got there. We stood along the wall in the back. An American flag hanging from the bare-girder ceiling wafted in the breeze created by large exhaust fans, and occasionally I felt a breath of cool, fresh air. But the big garage was too packed with people; it was stifling.

More people were still trickling in when we saw Mr. Sheehan, the police chief, the sheriff, and Mayor Gump enter through a side door that led to another part of the station. They sat along a metal table arranged at the front. Mayor Gump waved his hands for quiet. The steady roar of voices in conversation began to subside.

"Mr. Sheehan," the mayor told us in his high, reedy voice, "is the chairman of the emergency committee. We'll hear from him."

Sheehan got up. He was wearing brown coveralls and a baseball cap. His big voice boomed through the now-quiet garage. "I don't have to tell any of you that we have a serious problem." He glanced at a sheet of paper. "The level of the water out there right now is about eighteen feet, eight inches."

There was a chorus of groans. "What does that mean?" someone called.

"It means," Sheehan said, "trouble. Just like I said. The big flood in the thirties crested at nineteen feet."

Through more groans, his questioner up front asked, "Then we're about to get flooded again?"

"Not necessarily," Sheehan said. "For one thing, there's

been a lot of work on the banks since 1933. For another, we've got a good start. We've already put a couple of layers of sandbags all along the banks, and work is moving fast. The governor has promised us more manpower if he can find it. We're going to get some trustees from the penitentiary and some from BIS. We've got plenty of sand and plenty of bags. If the rain lets up, we can stay high and dry."

Someone asked, "How high is it supposed to go?"

"Well, we can't predict that for sure because it's still raining. We figure we can hold it with no trouble over twenty-one feet. At the rate the river is rising—"

"How fast is it rising?"

"It's been coming up about one inch every two hours. That means," Sheehan went on over some hubbub, "it could be as high as nineteen and a half or twenty feet by tomorrow this time. But by then we'll have another foot or two on the sandbags. So we think if everyone will pitch in and work like blazes, we can get through this with a little luck."

Voices rumbled everywhere. Someone called, "What's the highest it can go and not flood downtown?"

"We figure," Sheehan replied, "we can stay ahead of it to the twenty-three-foot mark. That gives us quite a margin. Barring some tremendous new rain upstream, we can make it—if, as I said, everyone pitches in.

"Now," he went on, "we've got emergency kitchens set up at the school, and workers will be able to rest and sleep in the Porterfield warehouse right down there near the work. For any families that need evacuation, the chief has a list of private homes that will put people up. We need more of you to sign up on that list if you have any room at all." He looked around, letting some of the conversation subside. "Harmony has been through some crises before, and we'll get through this one, too, as long as we all pull together."

Up near the front, Colonel Thatcher got to his feet. A few people booed.

"Go ahead, Colonel." Sheehan frowned.

"Mr. Mayor," the colonel said, "ladies and gentlemen, most of you know me. I'm the commandant of the camp outside town, here. We have more than four hundred able-bodied men out there who can be thrown into this battle."

"Keep 'em where they are!" someone called, and others whistled.

The colonel's face reddened. "We can guarantee heavy guard on the prisoners and their good behavior. I have spoken to some of the men out there, and I can assure you they are eager to help."

"The way they helped Sheehan's boy yesterday?" someone called. There was a chorus of grumbling agreement.

"Colonel," Sheehan said over the noise, "we appreciate your offer. We have already discussed it at length. Community feeling being what it is at this time, we decline your offer at this time."

There was ragged cheering. I saw my father's face darken.

"They're idiots," he fumed as we finally walked toward our car an hour later. "Look at that sky! That river could be out of all control by tomorrow this time. Don't they know the danger they're in?"

We reached the car, where Skipper heard us coming and started barking behind the closed glass. I spoke to him through the window and he calmed down. The cats were on the back shelf behind the rear seat.

My father unlocked the passenger-side doors. "I'm going to walk down and take a look. It's only a couple of blocks. Do you want to stay here?"

My mother nodded. "We'll wait in the car."

"Can I go?" I asked.

He hesitated. "Okay. You can go."

"Me!" Aggie said excitedly.

"Absolutely not. You stay with your mother."

Aggie frowned, climbed in the car, and started sucking her fingers. I asked if we could take Skipper, but my father said all we needed was a wet dog for the drive back home. So just he and I left the car and walked east, down the street past shops and repair garages, toward the river.

The rain pelted us lightly as we crossed the street at the next corner and proceeded by a line of small, shabby houses. Here the area began to look like a battleground. The streets were covered with the slime of sand and dirt spilled from trucks, and two dump trucks rumbled up the street, empty from unloading, as we proceeded. Cars were parked in helter-skelter confusion. At the next corner there were sawhorse barricades being manned by two of the town's constables. A few other people were walking down to take a look.

We moved around the corner of an old brick warehouse, where we could get our first broad view.

Where before there had been grassy strips and a gentle river meandering north to south, now there was a world of turgid water. The river already appeared at the top of the banks, and all along the crest of grass were rows of brown sandbags. Dumps of sand were everywhere, grayish figures of men shoveling the dirt into bags while others passed them man-to-man in a continuous line to where others on the banks were stacking them. I saw men slipping and sliding in the colossal quagmire.

The river itself appeared enormous. Brown, raging, carrying bits of tree limbs and other debris, it seemed to race past our position. Even at the distance of over two city blocks, its roar was incredible. I saw an entire tree, leaves still fresh, carried rapidly into our sight on the left, past us, and out of view downstream. Men in yellow raincoats—supervisors—yelled orders distantly and gave directions. I saw one worker throw down his shovel, walk over to a parked truck, and collapse in a heap against one of its tires. There was a Red Cross truck a block north. A line of men appeared to be getting coffee.

"Well, Squirt," my father said quietly, "that's what a flood looks like."

"I'd just as soon see it in a movie," I said.

He smiled grimly. "Let's head back."

We walked back uphill to the car, where Mother and Aggie waited with the pets. "It's bad," my father said. "It looks higher than twenty feet to me right now."

He started the car. We drove to the corner of Main Street and turned left. Poking along in traffic, we reached the edge of town. Ahead we saw a melee of cars and trucks, and some flashing red lights. Cars were turning around in the roadway and coming back.

"*Now* what?"

"Aren't they letting anyone through?"

"It doesn't look like it."

We inched to the front of the line. The red lights were on a highway patrol car. The trooper, rain streaming off his jacket, peered in the window at us. "I'm sorry, folks. You have to go back."

"We live out this way," my father told him.

"I'm sorry, sir. The bridge just went out up ahead. No way you're going to get home tonight, I'm afraid."

My father somberly backed around, and we started back for town.

"*Now* what do we do?" my mother asked. Her voice had a tinge of hysteria in it.

"Well, we'll just find one of those homes where they're putting people up. We don't have any choice, do we?"

"Oh dear!"

It took a while. Many other people, it appeared, had also been blocked from farms. There was a small crowd around the fire station. My father made me stay in the car this time while he went in. It was a very long wait. Finally he came out with a slip of paper in his hand.

The home where we were sent belonged to an older couple named Henderson. They were very nice. Mrs. Henderson said we could keep Skipper and the cats in the garage. Aggie and I took them out there and found a cozy dry frame building with a dirt floor. Mr. Henderson had some old tools hanging on the wall but no car, so there was lots of room. We got a carton for the cats, which they wouldn't stay in, and an old piece of rug for Skipper. When I told him to stay there, he curled up obediently, but I saw his blind eyes trying to follow the sounds of our departure all the way to the door, which we closed firmly.

In the house, which was very old-fashioned, Mrs. Henderson served us some sandwiches and tea. Mr. Henderson talked a lot about the railroad and being retired. They had been in Harmony during the earlier flood. They said it had been awful.

After we ate, my father said he would walk down to the river and volunteer to help. My mother clung to him as he hugged her at the door. He walked down the tree-shaded street in steady rain.

The Hendersons were nice and invited us into the living room to listen to the radio with them, but my mother herded Aggie and me upstairs to the bedroom they had given us. It had flowered wallpaper, lamps with beaded shades, and a great old canopy bed that swayed and creaked when you sat on it. Aggie played with some cards she had brought. My mother sat in an old rocker near the window and kept looking out while pretending to read her *Post*. I didn't know what to do, so I sat on the bed and swung my legs, making the springs creak. I thought of Skipper in the garage. I knew he was probably scared. I was scared, too.

15

In the dead of the night, with rain pelting lightly on the roof of the strange house that sheltered us, my father crept into the room. I was awakened not by his arrival but by my mother's whispers to him. She turned on one of the ornate old lamps near the bed and I saw him, wet and muddy, undressing and hanging the work clothes on metal hangers.

"It's coming up faster than they expected," he told her softly.

"Is it going to be all right?" she whispered back.

He shook his head and said nothing.

I pretended to be asleep as he got into bed with us. I felt the cold radiating from him. In moments his breathing became steady and deep, and my mother turned out the light again. I went back to sleep.

In the morning we were up early. The rain had stopped although clouds hung low over the town. Mrs. Henderson prepared a mammoth breakfast of eggs and bacon and toast, apologizing because she had no sugar for the tea. We sat around the big dining room table, with old, oval-framed pictures looking down at us, and ate while listening to the radio. In Sicily, General Patton was racing toward Palermo. There was flooding not only in Ohio but in parts of Indiana and Kentucky.

Borrowing an iron, my mother had iron-dried my father's work clothes, mud stains and all. He looked tired but guardedly cheerful.

"Today and tonight will tell the tale," he said. "It was over nineteen feet when I left in the middle of the night. But now the rain is slacking off. Maybe we'll be all right. It's going to be touch and go."

"If it's stopping, the river will go down," I said.

"Not necessarily," he explained. "Most of the rain that falls here will raise the river *below* Harmony. What we most have to worry about is what the weather is doing upstream."

"That's the way it was the last time, in thirty-three," Mrs. Henderson told us. "When the river crested here and went out of its banks, the sun was shining. Imagine that!"

"I'll get back down there," my father said. "I'll call and let all of you know how it looks."

"That won't be possible," Mr. Henderson said. "I'm afraid the telephone is out."

My father sighed.

"I'll go," I said. "Then I'll come back with the message." In actuality, I had been dying to think of an excuse to see the latest for myself.

"You'll just stay here," my mother said quickly.

"All I've got to do is go down with Dad and run back with what he tells me," I protested.

"He's right about that," my father said. "It might not be a bad idea."

"Sure!"

Frowning, my mother gave in. I rushed out to the garage and leashed Skipper, who was frisky and nervous after a night in unaccustomed surroundings. He obeyed me perfectly, however, heeling as we walked downtown with my father.

Thick clouds hung over the downtown section, its streets now coated with a tan slime from the sand trucks. My father first went to the fire station. We found Mr. Sheehan and Colonel Thatcher among the officials in the makeshift command center. A couple of soldiers were operating radios that seemed to broadcast mostly static, and others were studying maps and making telephone calls on the few lines still operational.

"Heard about your predicament, Davidson." The colonel frowned. "No problems at the camp. Probably both of us can do more good here."

"I knew we could probably get home by going around through Circleville," my father said, "but that would have taken a couple of hours."

"You did the right thing staying in town. We need every man we can get."

My father looked at Sheehan. "Does that mean we're going to use the prisoners?"

Sheehan scowled and ignored the question. "The river is rising a lot faster. We're at almost twenty feet. At the present rate, we'll be over twenty-three feet within six or seven hours."

"Isn't twenty-three as high as we can hold?"

"We may not get the walls that high. The workers are all exhausted. We've got eight or nine of them in the clinic, simply finished until they have time to recuperate."

"Then why not use the prisoners?" my father asked.

"We're not using the prisoners. Community feeling is too strong."

"Is community feeling stronger against the prisoners than against downtown being *flooded?*"

Sheehan's jaw set angrily. "We're getting the word out to evacuate a twelve-block area. Not many people living in it. Stores, mostly. The property damage will be terrible." He sighed. "I don't know if the town will ever be the same."

"I'll go down and see if I can help," my father said.

"Oh. George?"

My father looked at him, and Sheehan seemed a little embarrassed.

"Hardly a time to discuss this, George, but about the incident at your house."

My father watched him.

Sheehan frowned. "At home late last night I . . . had a little talk with my son. He had told his mother a few things he hadn't told me. I want you to know I don't blame your boy, here, for whatever happened. Bill admitted he threw a rock at the dog, here."

"That's why they were fighting," my father said.

"Yes. Well, I guess your boy misunderstood. Bill says the dog was watching him very suspiciously, and Bill thought he was about to attack."

"Is that what he said?" I piped up. "That Skipper was watching him suspiciously?"

"Yes."

"That's real strange, then!" I said triumphantly. I knelt beside Skipper and held his head up so Mr. Sheehan could get a clear look at his eyes. "You see these eyes? Skipper is *blind!*"

Sheehan's expression went blank. "God! Yes! I remember the night at your house now!"

"And he was tied up," I said. *"That's* why I was fighting Bill."

"I hardly have time now," Sheehan said with a low, angry tone. "But it looks like I have another talk coming with my boy."

"Maybe that wasn't the only misunderstanding," my father told him. "Rudi Gerhardt's actions have also been misunderstood and misinterpreted. Did you ever think of that?"

Sheehan ran his hand through his hair. "I just can't talk about it anymore right now! We're trying to save a town here!"

"All right." My father was angry. "What do you want me to do?"

"You can get a report from the crew bosses on how many men we have in each section. Any other messages they have, you can bring them back. We're having trouble with our communications."

"All right." He turned to me. "Go back to the Henderson house and tell them there's no immediate danger, we don't know much more than that, and I'll try to get by the house around the lunch hour. Okay?"

"Okay," I said eagerly. I caught Mr. Sheehan watching me. I

told him, "Rudi didn't mean to hurt anybody! He was trying to stop the fight between Bill and me, and that's the *truth!*"

Sheehan looked at me, harassed, and then turned away. Seeing the look in my father's eye, I gave Skipper a command and fled.

We followed orders precisely, as far as they had gone. I gave Mother and the Hendersons the message. But I was anxious to see the latest for myself, and I could not do that at the house. So after telling them the news, I turned and started back down the steps.

"Where are you *going?*" my mother called sharply.

"Back down there," I replied matter-of-factly.

Her brows knit. Evidently she thought I was still following orders. I was very busy looking innocent. She said nothing.

"Heel, Skipper," I ordered. And it worked! She let us leave again.

The lightest drizzle started coming down on us as we hurried along Main Street and to the intersection of Water Street. We hurried down toward the river. There were a couple of older men standing at barricades at Front Street and one of them hailed us as we started by.

"Where do you think you're going, kid?"

"I just saw Mr. Sheehan," I said. "We're carrying messages."

He frowned, removed a soggy baseball cap, and scratched his bald head. "Okay. Go ahead."

Strictly speaking, it had not been a lie. I had seen Sheehan, and if I saw my father, I intended to tell him the other messages had been delivered. Making sure Skipper stayed well heeled, I went on down into what increasingly looked like a combat zone.

Many of the piles of sand were gone now, shoveled up. It looked like not as many men were working as had been last night. The river was clearly higher. Looking across its turgid expanse, I could see places on the far side, near the dump, where water had gotten through and filled many low spots for what might have been acres. At the Red Cross station well to my left, almost out of sight around the river bend, a long line of

workers waited for coffee. Some buses below had BOYS INDUS-
TRIAL SCHOOL painted on their sides. The workers near the
buses were clearly boys, struggling to relay the heavy sandbags
to the top of the makeshift levee. I knew I was already in trouble, but the curiosity was too great. Moving between great, wet,
brown trucks, I crossed an area of storage for some kind of farm
machinery and down a cobbled street into the area on the level
of the sandbags and the roar of the river.

Down here it was warmer, the stink of the flood everywhere.
The pavement was slick underfoot from spilled sand and
seepage. The rumble of water made speech difficult. Men supervisors were urging boys along, keeping them at work although
they were clearly exhausted. Some of them were no bigger than
I was, and I was shocked that they could, two at a time, even
lift the heavy bags. To one side, a smaller group of the young-
sters, tough-looking kids, were resting on a heap of filled bags.
I scanned faces, and then my heart turned over.

"Hey, kid," Benny said wearily as I reached him. He was
slumped on some bags, smoking a cigarette. He was wet and
muddy and worn down like all the others. He looked older.

"Benny," I said. "Are you all right?"

"Sure," he said. He grinned, showing a gap where one of his
front teeth had been. "Some flood, huh? Maybe it'll get the
school."

"I went and saw your mom," I told him. "She said you were
okay."

"Yeah, she comes down sometimes, blubbers."

"Benny, are they treating you all right?"

"Sure. Great."

"I mean *really*."

He looked at me for what seemed a long time. "Sure," he
repeated finally, without the tough tone. "They're teaching me
how to be a mechanic."

"An automobile mechanic?"

"Sure."

"Hey. That's . . . great, Benny."

"Your mutt looks good. He still blind?"

"Yes. But he's learned everything fine. See? Say hello, Skipper."

Skipper wagged his tail.

Benny smiled. "I had a dog once. Only the guy that owned him came and took him back."

"When you get out, maybe you can have one. I—"

"The old lady is taking me somewhere else when I get out. There ain't likely to be no dog."

"You might get one, Benny. You never know."

For an instant his eyes became boyish. "That would be neat, wouldn't it?"

"Sure! Just ask your mom! I'll bet she'd say yes!"

A burly man in a brown uniform, carrying what looked like a short baseball bat, strode up. "Okay, guys! Back to it, now!" He slapped the little bat in the palm of his hand.

Benny, like the others, scrambled up. "See you, kid," he said.

"I hope you do good as a mechanic, Benny," I told him.

He looked sharply at me. "Huh?"

"I said I hope you do good as a mechanic."

He showed the gap in his teeth again. "Are you kidding me? I ain't gonna be no stupid mechanic. I'm gonna be a bank robber."

"Move it, Harrison!" the big man ordered angrily.

"Aah, your mother's mustache," Benny growled under his breath, and moved along with his pals to resume work.

I watched him trudge back to the top of the levee. A bigger boy took a sandbag from another and staggered under its weight. Benny shook his head patiently, shoved the bigger boy out of the way, grabbed the bag, and hurled it to the next person in line with the velocity of a shot. I glanced at the brawny supervisor. He had seen it, too. A little grin ghosted across his face and was gone.

Benny was all right. He would stay all right. They weren't going to get him down, ever.

Feeling depressed and bereft, I wandered north along the levee. There was an area, a sort of command post, where crude wooden steps had been built onto the top of the rising sandbag wall. I climbed up onto it and found a platform, without railings and extending over the rushing water. Beyond the edge of the platform, a yellow-and-red post protruded from the muddy water, constantly shaken by its force. Large black numbers were painted on the post. The lowest number I could see, about six inches above the water, was 21.

Feeling the platform tremble beneath my feet, I clung tightly to Skipper's leash and looked around me. I could see the river frighteningly wide and wild to my left and right. To the left it curved out of sight a half mile away, details hidden by the humidity, haze, and continuing light drizzle. To my right it went under the bridge, almost covering the central section now, passed the grain elevator and the warehouses, and bent again, out of my view. So the little measuring platform had been installed at the center of the curve that the river would cut if it rose beyond the puny efforts of the community to hold it back.

Standing there and feeling the pressure of the mighty rush of water, I wondered how anyone imagined they could possibly win this battle. Although there were many workers, they were stretched thin along the line of battle. I could see similar activity, on a lesser scale, on the far side, but there the fight had already been partially lost and the low ground was more swamped than it had been only minutes earlier. I wondered if Benny's mother's house would be flooded. I wondered if Benny had thought of it.

"What are you doing up here!" an angry voice exploded close by. A hand grabbed my shoulder painfully, turning me. It was my father, with Mr. Sheehan and some others coming up the steps behind him. My father looked terrifically angry. He shook me. "Don't you know you could fall off of this thing and get yourself *killed?*"

"I was being careful!" I protested.

"What's this boy doing up here?" Mr. Sheehan demanded.

"That's what I was trying to find out."

One of the others was Mayor Gump. He had walked forward to get a view of the level post. "Look at that!" he exclaimed excitedly.

The others turned as Colonel Thatcher and the police chief climbed the stairs.

"My God," Sheehan said. "That's up two inches in less than thirty minutes."

"All that rain in Columbus last night. It's going to go twenty-five feet."

For an instant no one spoke. I read their expressions. Harmony was doomed. As if to punctuate that certainty, the platform trembled under the force of the Big Walnut.

"I don't see what more we can do," Sheehan said after another long minute. "We'll have to give it up, Mr. Mayor. Pull everyone back to safety."

"Downtown will *go!*" Mayor Gump cried.

"There's nothing more we can do."

"There's one more thing you can do," my father told them sharply.

They turned to him. His face was grimmer than I had ever seen it.

"That's right," he said. "I mean our prisoners."

"We've been through that time and again, George!"

"And they might still save the town, damn it!"

"We can't afford," Mayor Gump said shrilly, "to have our community ruined by—"

"It's going to be wrecked anyway by this river! What do *any* of you have to lose by giving it this last try?"

I saw Sheehan look at the mayor. The mayor's face twisted. He did not reply. Colonel Thatcher and the police chief said nothing. Again the platform trembled.

"Look!" my father said heatedly. "Every man we've got out here is exhausted! They look like they're working in slow motion! But the people in Columbus said it's not raining up there now. If we could just hold through today, we might get the crest. The river might start to recede. We've got more than four hundred fresh, strong, willing men out there at that camp! Are you going to stand by and let Harmony literally go under, or are you going to put aside your hate long enough to make this one last try?"

Sheehan said slowly, "We have no assurance we can win anyway."

"If you don't try using our men, you know you've lost! Why not at least *try?*"

Sheehan looked at the mayor. The older man licked his lips, and his eyes sagged with a kind of defeat. "The people would never like it."

"How much do you think they're going to like being *flooded?*"

Mayor Gump looked back at the level pole, back at my father, then at Colonel Thatcher. "How long would it take to transport men here?"

"Two hours," the colonel snapped. "The Krauts are fresh. They can work around the clock if necessary."

Mayor Gump's shoulders drooped. He told Sheehan, "I'm willing to go along with whatever—"

Sheehan cut in, "Get them here, Colonel. It's the only chance we've got left."

The colonel turned to my father. "There's a line open at the fire station, Davidson."

"Yes, sir!" my father snapped, heading for the steps. "You come with me!" he barked at me.

We rushed down the steps and I had to run to keep up with his long strides as we hurried uphill toward the fire station, past the barricades.

"Dad!" I panted. "Dad!"

"What?" he answered, distracted.

"Rudi, too!" I begged.

"What?"

"Rudi, too! Make sure they let Rudi out to come, too!"

"I don't know about Rudi." He scowled. "The people are afraid of these prisoners. Rudi, if he's recognized, would scare them worst of all after what they think he did."

"What do they think he would do?" I demanded derisively. "Escape?"

"He might. Any of them might."

I simply could not hold it back any longer. "They could have *all* escaped any time they wanted to, Dad."

"Don't talk nonsense. There's no time."

"There's a sewer system under the camp," I told him. "It dumps out in the creek just below our house. I've explored it. I've walked it right from the creek and climbed right up inside the camp."

He bent over, staring, and veins stood out on his forehead. *"What?"*

"I didn't know where I was going," I admitted. "But I climbed up and came out in that courtyard-type place."

"You?" His eyes were bulging.

"Me," I snapped.

"What *happened?*"

"The prisoners grabbed me."

"They—!"

"Sure. They were scared half to death! They knew about the sewer right from the start, but they were afraid if they told you or the colonel, they'd be in trouble. So they've hid it all this time, hoping like mad you didn't find out."

"You . . . got inside the camp through a sewer?" my father said, striving to digest it. "And *they* know about it?"

"You should have seen 'em," I said. "They were scared to death I would tell. But I didn't. And I wouldn't be telling now if it wasn't for Rudi. *He* knew, Dad. All the time. Just like the bald German that sort of bosses the rest of them around in there. They made me promise not to tell, and then Rudi took me back to the creek."

"When," my father asked huskily, "did all this happen?"

"Right after that iceman hit a prisoner and you had the meeting at the house and they all said how dangerous the prisoners were."

My father stared. His expression changed from disbelief to incredulity, and then his mouth began to twitch. "You—went in—?" He bent over and began to choke. Then he began to laugh. The tears rolled down his cheeks. "All our wonderful security!" he managed. "All our planning! And you—it's too good!"

I watched him laughing, and everyone around us stared as if he had gone mad. "So what about Rudi?" I demanded.

"I'll let him come," my father choked, still convulsed with laughter. "I'll let them all come. Hell, why not?" He banged me on the back. "Squirt, you're priceless! Come on! I've got to make a phone call." Still laughing, he led me away.

16

After he made his telephone call, my father told me to go to the Henderson house, report what was happening, and stay there. I obeyed the first part of his instructions but forgot the second part.

"What are *you* doing here?" he demanded angrily almost two hours later when he caught me serving coffee at the Red Cross station.

"They need help!" I told him, and thrust a cup at him.

He rolled his eyes heavenward, took the coffee, and hurried away.

The first prisoner trucks started arriving at noon. Guards piled out, then the Germans. At once, some of the German prisoners began forming up their men and yelling orders in their own language. The other workers looked on dully, not fully comprehending. The guards got back out of the way. Prisoners, formed into squads, ran into positions. Bags began to be passed at a record pace. I did not see Rudi but knew he was somewhere nearby. With new men on the line, we were deluged at the coffee station as haggard farmers stumbled up for a brief rest.

The trucks continued to rumble in and disgorge more workers. After an hour or so, almost every man active on the lines was in prisoner fatigues. Engines coughed into action and prisoners, on their own volition, manned graders to move piles of sand closer to the levee. Fresh rows of sandbags, not yet stained by the river, began to pile on the temporary wall.

"They're no dummies!" one of the farmers told another in my hearing. "One of them told Sheehan they ought to take *down* some of the works on the far side—let it spill into the bottoms over there to ease the pressure on this side. They're doing it. Somebody said the level over here hasn't gone up for thirty minutes now."

"What happens to the houses and stuff over there in the bottoms?" his companion asked blankly.

"It's getting flooded, I'm afraid, but—"

"Leave it to the Krautheads," the other man cut in angrily, "to figure out a way to start some of the flooding right away!"

Thunder rolled overhead and light rain resumed. The word was that no new rain was falling to the north. The prisoners appeared to take no rest breaks. They were all here now, and as much German as English was heard in shouted questions and instructions. The guards had long since put their rifles aside and were working side by side with the men they were supposed to guard. I heard reports secondhand. The pole beside the platform showed 22. It was holding steady. Now it was up another two inches. Someone was hurt. An ambulance came, siren winding down, red lights flashing as it crept through the chaos. Someone said it was raining again in Columbus. Someone else said that was a false report.

By four o'clock, I was exhausted like most of the men. Some women appeared at the Red Cross station with piles of fresh-baked doughnuts. I let them replace me on the coffee line, untied Skipper where he had been tied so long outside, and went searching for Rudi and/or my father.

There was just too much going on to find either of them eas-

ily. New truckloads of sand were being delivered. The levee
had sprung some leaks here and there, and men were trying to
patch things up. The BIS buses had been moved and a couple
of flatbed trucks pulled in, loaded with sacks of grain. Men
were slashing the sacks, dumping the golden grain into the
mud, refilling them with sand. I saw Mayor Gump and Mr.
Sheehan on the observation platform jutting out over the water
from the levee. Sheehan spied me at the same moment and
waved for me to come up and join them. Puzzled, I climbed the
rickety wooden stairs to the platform, which trembled under the
weight of the rushing water close below.

"Son, where's your father?" Sheehan asked worriedly.

"I don't know. I think he's back working nearer the coffee
tent—"

"Find him. Get him back here." Sheehan pointed at the
marker pole jutting out of the muddy water nearby. "It's still
rising."

I looked. The lowest number I could now read was 23.
"What can my *dad* do?"

Mayor Gump said, "We have to start evacuating parts of
downtown. Your father has to get some of the prisoners together—help people move out. Tell him that. Tell him we'll wait
right here to talk with him about it." The mayor's face worked.
"Tell him . . . there isn't a moment to lose."

I looked upstream toward the distant coffee tent, the melee
of trucks and workers below the sandbag wall. I spied my father's familiar figure perhaps a hundred yards away. He was
atop the levee, pointing and issuing orders to hard-working
prisoners. The roar of the river and all the confusion between
us made signaling him impossible.

"I'll get him," I promised.

"Hurry," Mr. Sheehan said.

I plunged down the slippery wooden stairs and into the
muddy chaos below the wall. Pulling Skipper along on his
leash, I ran the distance, arriving below my father's working
position badly out of breath. The sandbag wall here was much
broader at its base than on top, so that some of the men were
ignoring ladders thrown against it and were climbing the

slanted sides at their work. The wall was thicker here, too. I knew my father was on top, but I could not see him from below.

"*Dad!*" I called. My voice was swallowed up.

There was no time to lose. With Skipper coming up after me, loosely leashed, I scrambled up the slimy, gritty wall of bags. Reaching the top, I saw my father out on the brink, directing some prisoners who were stacking fresh bags in an apparent small fault in the levee. Staggering on the wet and uneven bags, I hurried toward him.

"Dad! Mr. Sheehan said—"

"What are you doing here?" my father demanded, whirling angrily. "Get back, Squirt! This whole thing is shaky!"

I dropped Skipper's leash. "Skipper. Stay." I went forward to my father. "Dad! Mr. Sheehan and the mayor want to see you right away! They're down on the platform. They said they need some prisoners to help evacuate the—"

I got no further. I had reached my father's side, and just as he reached a steadying hand toward me, I stepped on a sandbag perilously near the edge. The bag shifted under my weight. I lost my balance. I think I yelled as I tried to catch his hand. I missed. My feet slid from under me and there was a sickening instant of fall and then I tipped over the edge, tumbling out over the water.

"*Squirt!*" I heard my father cry despairingly.

I hit hard, the water shockingly cold. My eyes were open and all I saw for a moment was a world of swirling brown bubbles. I tasted the muddy water, choking. Then I bobbed up, being turned rapidly around by the force of the current.

The force was terrifying, whirling me out away from the sandbag wall. I saw my father's face above me, etched in shock and fear. He was crying something. The water spun me and I fought, but I was never a good swimmer.

"*Help!*" I yelled. And then: "*Skipper!*"

From the top of the wall a blur of tan and black moved. I saw my dog leap blindly off the edge of the wall. He plunged down, hitting with a great splash. I saw his head come up; his sightless eyes seemed frightened.

"Skipper! Here, boy! This way! Help!"

He heard me and swam strongly toward me. We were both being carried with terrifying speed downstream. Behind us, at least two men hit the water, trying to catch us. I saw at once that they were already out of range. Distant voices came. I was dimly aware of other men yelling and running atop the wall, which was now more than thirty feet away. I was mainly watching Skipper. I kept yelling. He swam strongly, head up, fighting the river that seemed able to toss me in any direction at its whim.

My head went under water. I started to strangle, and fought with all the remaining strength in my arms and legs. The cold had begun to sap me. I went under again and choked, almost vomiting. I was not going to make it. The river was too strong.

"Skipper!"

He was close. With a final brave lunge he reached me, banging his thick, matted wet fur into my face. I clutched at him and tangled my fingers in his coat. Instantly his strength seemed to flow through me. I could feel the powerful lunging motions of his legs and he started working to keep both of us afloat. *It isn't fair,* I thought. *I'll just drown him, too.* But I was helpless without him. I clung, coughing and fighting for air.

We seemed to hurtle along at great speed. I could not see clearly, but knew when we flashed past the raised observation platform. Men on top moved violently and something like a great snake—a coil of rope—was hurled through the air toward us. It hit the brown water just ahead of us with a sprinkling splash. Releasing one hand's grip in Skipper's coat, I lunged for it—and missed. I felt the stout rope brush my flailing legs as we were carried past.

Skipper, blind, knew none of this. His head was up and he was gasping for air. My weight kept tugging his muzzle into the water, but he kept lunging valiantly, raising us both higher again. I saw to my despair that his efforts were actually carrying us a bit farther into the center of the raging stream, away from the waving, shouting men atop the levee. I tried feebly to tug at him, making his head turn toward the bank. It was no use. The river turned us completely around so that for a moment all I saw was the vast, turgid expanse of the river, and then the bridge far ahead, and then, blurrily, the sandbag wall again. A terrifyingly huge tree, its branches still fully leafed out, sailed close to us in a spray of foam and smaller debris.

"Skipper, go to the right!" I pleaded. "To the *right!*" But of course this was not an order he had been taught, and perhaps he was too frightened—and fast wearying—to obey anyway. He knew it was my voice in his ears, the weight of my body tugging him downward in this terrible unfamiliar universe. All he knew to do was fight for our lives, and he was doing that with everything in him.

We turned again, swirling in the current. The big tree was a little ahead. Skipper made a choking sound, a cough or a sneeze, and began swimming more spasmodically. I saw men leaping into the water off to what was now our left. Then we spun around again and they were on the right, and more men were hitting the water up ahead of us. My hands were knots of pain in Skipper's thick fur. All sensation seemed to have fled from my legs. *How was Skipper keeping us up?*

Without warning, something big and dark loomed into my vision—the great broken end of a log. I saw its mass over us and then the water drove it down upon us. I felt the shuddering impact as it hit Skipper's side, driving both of us under for a few seconds. Then we popped back up again and I saw bright red on my hands in my dog's fur, and his swimming movements were all disconnected now, failing. I could feel his strength go, the river start to take us under.

Voices dinned in my ears—voices yelling in German. I fought my head out of the water again with my last ounce of energy. There were faces in the water all around me. I recognized Rudi. Strong hands grasped me. I was borne up. Ropes hissed into the water around us. More hands grasped my body, and the German shouts of coordination surrounded me. I saw Rudi grasp a heavy dark rope, felt it snaked around my middle, sawing at me roughly.

The ropes pulled us toward the embankment. Perhaps I lost consciousness for a few seconds, because the next thing I knew, men were reaching down from the top of the wall, were grabbing me and the others, pulling us up and out of the water. I was hauled out bodily and slung onto the slippery, blessedly solid sandbags. I choked, retching. Hands pounded my back painfully and I vomited, a stream of brown water coming up. Rudi, hugging me, sat me up. Water streamed off of us.

"You are safe!" he told me. "You are safe!"

Through the wall of bedraggled men around us, my father broke through. He too was soaked and wild-eyed. Seeing me, he threw himself to his knees and hugged me with Rudi. "Thank God!" he rasped. "You're okay now! You're—"

"It was Skipper, Dad," I shuddered. "Skipper held me up. He saved my life until the other guys could—" I stopped suddenly, sitting bolt upright. "*Skipper!*"

Rudi jumped to his feet. "The dog?" he yelled at the other men. With an oath, he pushed them roughly aside, opening a view to the rushing river. He stared.

The river was empty of life.

"*Skipper!*" I screamed despairingly.

"Downstream!" Rudi told the men. "Run and look everywhere! Pass the word!"

Men scrambled, shouting. My father stared at me. "He'll be all right. He—"

"A log hit us," I said. "*Find* him, Dad! He's hurt! Go help! *Please!*"

"I can't leave you, Squirt—"

"*Dad!*"

He let me go then and hurried away. I sat hunched over, teeth chattering. But the chill went deeper even than my aching body. They had to find him. They had to.

It was forever before my father came back. His face told the story.

"We'll keep looking," he said. "He could have crawled out— might have gone farther downstream. We'll have people looking until we find him."

I did not speak. There were no words. I stared at the horrid river, its emptiness. The cold shook me from head to toe, and I knew.

He was gone.

17

The river crested late that day at twenty-three feet, four inches. The levees held. Harmony was saved. I was not there when workers finally saw the line on the measurement post finally start to recede, and a great cheer went up along the battle line. I had been rushed to the Henderson house, where I was covered with high-piled blankets and fed tea and toast until I fell into an exhausted sleep.

In the morning the skies were cloudy, but without new rain. My father sternly ordered me to remain in bed and hurried downtown. My mother made sure the orders this time were obeyed. Aggie sat on the edge of the bed with her frayed blanket, sucking her fingers and watching me with solemn eyes. The Hendersons poked in and out periodically, trying to cheer me. I felt faint and feverish and inconsolable.

"You can get another puppy," my mother told me.

"No," I said. "Never."

She smiled. "You'll feel differently later."

"No!"

After a few hours my father came back. He entered the bedroom cautiously, as if afraid of what he might find. My mother quietly left the room, taking Aggie with her. I put down my "Captain Marvel" comic.

"Well, Squirt," my father said wearily, sitting on the edge of the bed, "it's already down below nineteen feet. Looks like we won."

"*Won?*" I repeated bitterly.

"Son, I wish there was something I could say."

I stared at him, waiting to hear verification of what I already knew.

He sighed and his forehead wrinkled. "We've searched both banks. We had Boy Scouts out this morning as far down as Circleville. We've looked everywhere."

"He's dead," I said. "I killed him."

"Maybe he's still alive. We've asked people farther south—"

"No. He's dead. I killed him."

My father's face twisted. "You didn't kill him."

I looked at him. There was nothing to say.

He smoothed the hair off my forehead. "It's okay to cry, you know."

I stared at him, dry-eyed.

"Sometimes," he said gently, "it helps."

I picked up my comic—stupid comic—again. I looked at the brightly colored pictures and meaningless words. There was nothing inside me. All I could feel was a vast, echoing cold.

There were whispered consultations. The doctor came again, and then I could hear more whispers in the hallway. Beyond the windows the sun beamed. I knew they were worried about me, but that was meaningless, too. I put down my comic and closed my eyes and again felt the cold thickness of Skipper's fur in my wet hands, and saw the bright splash of his blood. His blood was on my hands.

In the coming weeks my family tried very hard. I stayed indoors at home, worked in desultory fashion at a model, and cleaned out every memory of Skipper. I took his box to the trash dump, pulled his stake out of the yard, went down and hurled his ball as deep as I could throw it into the woods.

"Maybe we could get another dog," my mother said one night at the supper table. I didn't answer her. I could only stare. I thought she was insane.

I hated it, the way they watched me, pretending to be cheerful as if nothing was wrong. I stayed away from them as much as possible, in my room or sitting hidden inside the mouth of the drainage pipe that led to the camp. News registered on me, as when the bridge was repaired between our home and town, or when the civic celebration of the town's deliverance from the flood was announced and scheduled for late July. But nothing really affected me.

"You can cry," my mother told me one day.

"Why?" I shot at her bitterly.

"You have to let it go, darling. You have to go on."

"Why?"

They made me go with them to the civic celebration. Main Street was roped off around the park, and more than half the town turned out. Under the hot July sun a band played patriotic songs and twirlers twirled. The mayor made a speech and so did the colonel. There were American flags for everyone, whirligigs for the children. A squad of the German prisoners attended, standing stiffly at attention during the speeches and then staying to themselves near their truck.

In his speech, Mayor Gump made it sound like our prisoners were all really Americans who got their birthplace mixed up. There was a lot of cheering over this. It sounded wrong to me. In my solitude, I had pondered it. I knew that most of our prisoners were good men, victims of politics and accident of birthplace. I knew that their efforts, bordering on heroism, had probably saved the town. But Nazi Germany was still a fact. Some of these men had voted for Hitler. They were not all good men. This fact puzzled and confused me, but in my present state of mind it did not seem to matter much—was just another puzzle that I would never understand or much care about again.

Rudi was among the prisoner honor group. I saw him glancing at me repeatedly during the special ceremony. This involved a marble obelisk, about six feet tall, with a bronze plaque on its gleaming side. It commemorated the flood. On the bottom of the plaque were the names of all the Germans who had helped. The mayor said the obelisk would stand forever, like the American Way of Life. Everyone applauded and then the band played "The Stars and Stripes Forever."

Afterward people milled around. I refused an ice cream cone. My parents edged me toward the prisoners at their truck, and Rudi was standing there.

"So," he said with a faint, caring smile. "I hear you have been sick."

"I'm fine," I told him.

"You are thin."

I shrugged.

"We have something for you," Rudi said. He signaled to one of his companions, who went to the back of the truck. He took out a fairly large carton, the top open, and carried it to Rudi. Smiling, Rudi reached into the box and took out a squirming little black German shepherd puppy.

He thrust it toward me. "For you."

I pulled back in horror. *"No!"*

Rudi's smile faded. He continued to hold the wriggling pup. "But he is for you. From us. With our gratitude."

"No! I'll never have another dog! I don't *want* any other dog!"

"Squirt," my father said huskily beside me, "take this puppy. You—"

"No! I don't want him! I don't want the responsibility! I don't want *never* to train something—love something—and lose it again!"

"You must love again," Rudi told me. "This is living."

"I don't have to and I won't! Ever! You just love something and then you lose it and it's all a gyp!"

My mother put her arm around me, bending, then kneeling beside me. Her eyes were filled with concern. "Darling, you loved Skipper. That—"

"And I *killed* him!" I cried.

"You gave him life," my father said.

"I gave him nothing! All I did was get him killed!"

"He was blind. *Blind*. You gave him your love and you made his one summer a—a paradise. Squirt! Don't you see? Because of you, he had far, *far* more life than most animals ever do, even if they live to be a hundred! You gave him a grand life, son, and he gave his life back for you. If he could have chosen, he would have *chosen* it."

I stared at them in turn—at the squirming little puppy still in Rudi's outstretched hands. I wanted no more of this pain, no more of such risk. But something beyond any of their words— something in their very love for me that radiated from each of them into the cold of my depths—mingled with the words and I felt a great clotted pain deep inside begin to break loose.

Rudi extended the puppy closer. "Take him. See? He loves you already. Neither of you can help yourselves."

Without my willing it, my hands reached out. Rudi thrust the puppy into my arms. I tried to harden my heart. The little dog went into convulsions of joy, licking my face frantically, nipping at my ears. I hugged him close. In his delirium of joy, the puppy wet himself, a hot stream against the front of my shirt. I buried my face in his rich puppy fur and hugged him against me so tightly I thought I would pull his warmth completely inside my own body. And then suddenly, I was weeping as I had never wept in my life.

Holding my new dog—my new Skipper—and crying with a wracking sense of relief and salvation made the warmth of new life inside me feel like the heat of the sun itself.

Epilogue

In the fall the prisoners were moved to another work camp in Kentucky, and my father's new job took us to Washington. It was many years before I again visited Harmony. The small obelisk still stood in place, heavier traffic now beating around the square, the bronze plaque green-gray with the years. I went by the old school but it was gone, replaced by a new building of steel and glass. I found Jimmy Cantwell in his drugstore, and he told me that Bill Sheehan was president of the bank now, and Phil Inright, when a high school senior, had died in a terrible car accident. He had heard that Benny Harrison was in the Army, a career man much decorated in Korea.

Our old house in the country was still there. They had a garden in the same spot where we had tried to grow one. As I stopped the car, an Irish setter ran out toward the road and barked at me, and I saw a small boy in the side yard, swinging in a swing made from an old tire. I drove on.

My own business, that of a reporter, took me many places in the next years, but it was not until the late 1970s that I finally went to Germany. My wife secretly considered me a very great fool as I consulted the telephone directory in Munich. There were many Gerhardts, but only one listed as a veterinarian in a nearby community.

On a sunny Sunday afternoon we drove out of the beautiful city into the rolling countryside. On an isolated mountain road we found a house with a steep Bavarian roof and windowboxes ablaze with geraniums. As I walked around our car to open the door for my wife, a stooped, gray-haired, but unmistakable figure came around the house from the garden. Beside him, sharply at heel, was a handsome shepherd who might have been the twin of my own long-lost Skipper, or the dog who replaced him in my life if never entirely in my heart.

"You see?" I told my wife. "He is still alive. He had to be."

She walked beside me to the garden gate and toward the old man. His smile had not changed in the slightest.

"Welcome," he said. "I have been waiting for you."

We clasped hands.

About the Author

Jack M. Bickham, a professor of journalism at the University of Oklahoma, has written over fifty books, including *Baker's Hawk* and *Dinah, Blow Your Horn,* both of which were *Reader's Digest* Condensed Book selections. The widely shown Walt Disney Productions film *The Apple Dumpling Gang* was based on one of his novels.